Christian

Hope you enjoy this
Best Regards.

Dr. Wayne E Haly
4/2000

THE LAST FERRY TO CLOVER BAY

THE LAST FERRY TO CLOVER BAY

DR. WAYNE E. HALEY

Quiveir Press

TACOMA

Published by Quiveir Press
702 Court A, Bodega Court Building
Tacoma WA 98402
(253) 272.7105

Library of Congress Catalogue Card Number: 98-67013
1. Fiction I. Title

ISBN: 0-9661247-1-5

Cover Art and Book Design by Susan Givens

Manufactured in the United States of America by
Gorham Printing, Rochester WA

10 9 8 7 6 5 4 3 2 1

Dedication

This book is dedicated to the real
Royal Lady Lydia of the Stygian Triangle,
Kathleen,
without whom this book would have
never been written.

Acknowledgment

So many people helped with this
project, that I know I cannot mention
them all. But I do wish to thank the following:
Dr. Pamela McCauley, Dr. Leonard Cabianca,
Dr. William E. "Wiley P." Post, Dr. Lester Giesel,
Dr. Daniel Brannum, and Larry, Jerry, Gordon,
David and Mercedes though they now live
in a different dimension.

I would also like to thank Susan Givens, my editor
and especially Marge Christensen of MUFON,
for her friendship and expertise.

THIS IS A QUIVEIR PRESS BOOK.

The word *Quiveir* is the old Norman spelling for the word we know as quiver. It is defined as either a case for holding and carrying arrows, or as the arrows in the case.

Books published by Quiveir Press are like arrows. They fly from the author's imagination into the bookmaking process and finally out into the world. Like arrows, the author's ideas and images are intended to pierce the reader's mind. Each book published by Quiveir Press aims to enrich lives by creating appreciation for both the content and the ongoing delight of the printed word.

Designed by the Venetian printer Aldus Manutius and dating back to the Italian Renaissance, Bembo typeface was used for this book. It is known for its sense of classic timelessness.

PREFACE

"It was the best of times; it was the worst of times." What a truly engaging way to start a book, but since some upstart of an Englishman has already used that sentence, one must begin, instead, by saying that it was the worst of times and it was the worst of times. This was especially true in Clover Bay, Washington on the island known as Wibley.

The difference between a recession and a depression is whether one has a job or not. The Shrub was still President and the Duck was V.P.; both still living in Washington, D.C., and making the free world safe for corporate thieves, big business and the almighty American dollar. The economy was still bad. The boundaries of the world map were still changing, and everything was pretty much messed up as usual. And it had been thus ever since the country had decided to stay cool with Coolidge in '28.

This story is not about the power brokers in New York, Washington, or London, but rather about a group of people that came to live on an island just a little north of Seattle and a little west of reality. It is about how one night, in a fit of rage, and being so small in such an immense universe, this group decided to do something about all of it — to hit back just once for the little guy, for the man on the street. It was just like something out of an old Jimmy Stewart movie, only the results were slightly different. But that is getting ahead of the story.

So, with the reader's approval, the author will take some liberties and tell you a bit about each of the five individuals, the place where they live, and why they decided one wet fall night to do something which could change, at least for the moment, the course of recorded history.

CHAPTER 1

Clover Bay is, in reality, two bays that adjoin each other. The true Clover Bay is the southernmost of the bays, and runs east through north to northwest until it meets up with Useless Bay. Useless Bay was named such because at high tide the water in the Bay was maybe a foot and a half deep, and at low tide the water was merely six inches. Not enough water resides in Useless Bay to float anything except perhaps a small dinghy or a rubber raft. So, the old timers in the area decided that it was useless for any of their activities, and being men of vision and understanding they named it so.

Clover, on the other hand, is a deep-water bay. It has been home port to a whole list of great and not so great sailing ships since the mid 1800s. The ships have carried lumber and processed fish, and a lot of people have been going and coming ever since those early days. But gradually, as things changed, new harbors sprang up and different routes were chosen. In the process, Clover Bay slowed its once rapid beat to a middle-aged pulse. It still had the fishing industry and the processing plants, which kept a good economy in the town, but around 1949 a strange thing happened. A Pacific Ocean warm-water current called El Niño moved two hundred miles further south down the coastline of Chile. All the fish in the island district of Wibley moved a hundred miles south to the coastline of central Washington and Oregon. So, the processing plants closed, and most of the fishing fleet either moved north to Anacortes to kill the salmon, or south to the harbor at Newport in Oregon to hunt the cod.

However, there were still some die-hard fishermen that would not quit Clover Bay, and they continued hunting the sparse fishing grounds for enough of a catch to keep them alive and their boats afloat.

CHAPTER 2

Margaret Twitchell lived her entire 84 years in the State of Washington, on Wibley Island. Her family home had been her pride and joy for most of those years. The five acres of cranberry fields that stretched from the house to the water's edge on Useless Bay were always a delight to behold. The mixture of red and green colors reflecting on the backdrop of the blue water of the Bay was a painter's palette to behold.

The old house with its twelve rooms, basement, and three outbuildings, was typical for this edge of the world. Wild berry vines would have grown up the side of the shop building almost totally engulfing it if Margaret was not out there with her pruning shears twice a year. It had been these very vines that had cost the old girl her life.

One day while trying to correct their errant ways, she was hacking and cutting away in the heat of the summer. In Washington, that is about 62 degrees.

People were drinking lemonade and talking about the heat wave and hoping for the return of the rain. Anyway, there she was working away at disciplining those vines, when suddenly she had the first formal physics lesson of her lifetime. Basically, she learned that one cannot defy the natural laws of gravity. As she extended her reach three feet beyond the center of gravity from a ten-foot-tall ladder, the mass of her body hung out over ten feet of empty space with nothing to support her. Suddenly she knew what Galileo had discovered when he dropped two balls from the leaning tower of Pisa. The major difference: Galileo was tried as a heretic; Margaret Twitchell fell at terminal velocity — to coin a phrase.

The folks in the little town of Clover Bay had a nice little funeral. Clyde Lindsey, the local lawyer and escapee from the urban blight of southern California, took care of the probate and the handling of the will. It seemed that Margaret's only relative was a nephew in Naples, Florida. He was balding and fat, and his only interest at all in the old family homestead was that of telling Clyde that he wanted the best deal that the lawyer could get for it. And he wanted it as soon as possible.

Clyde didn't have a lot of lawyering to do around Clover Bay, so he figured he could afford the time to become the real estate agent for the old place. Besides, he could probably make a buck or two in the process. So, being a creature of habit, Clyde put an ad in the Seattle, Portland, San Francisco and Los Angeles papers:

NICE FIXER-UPPER on Useless Bay. 5 acres of cranberries, 8 bedrooms, 1 bath, 3 outbuildings. Needs tender loving care and $80,000.00 cash.

Well, a couple of weeks went by and Clyde checked the post office every day. Nothing came showing itself. He would talk to Mildred, the Postmaster. They would complain about the heat (it was up to 68 degrees), and then he'd walk back to his office and shuffle through the stack of papers that he had shuffled through the day before. He'd look out his front bay window at the small harbor and then wonder what he was going to do that evening.

This day, however, his reverie was interrupted by the ringing phone, which was nothing more than a dust collector on his desk.

"Clyde Lindsey, Attorney at Law, how may I help you?" The silence at the other end of the phone was deafening, "Hello, Hello?"

A voice that sounded like a cross between Orson Wells and John Wayne boomed across the invisible span of time and space. "You answer your own phone, for Christ's Sake! Are you a machine or am I talking to a real person?"

"I am real; how may I help you, sir?" Clyde was doing his best Andy Hardy routine.

"Don't call me 'sir.' I work for a living." The voice had a hollow sound to it. "Listen, the house you put in the paper, where is it?"

"Who am I speaking with, please?" Some of the

Washington-grown charm was wearing thin, and a little of the L. A. chrome was starting to show through.

"Lawyers answer a question with another question. Jesus! Is the house on the water or does it have access to the water?"

"It's on the Bay, but the Bay is too shallow there for a boat, if that's what you have in mind. Who is this?" — a little more determination in the voice.

"If you're planning to change careers and become 'a mind reader, think about it some more. You're lousy at it, fellow." The voice went on and drifted into space.

"Look, I want to know to whom I am speaking, or else I shall discontinue this conversation." Clyde suddenly felt the old self return.

"Calm down, sport. Okay if I send you a check for the place and you FedEx the paperwork back to me? FedEx. You can do that, can't you?" The voice goaded into the lawyer's mind.

"Of course, I can. What the hell do you think I am, anyway? Now, who the hell are you?"

"Mallory, Doc Mallory. I'll send the check tomorrow and get the papers the day after, right?"

"Okay." Lindsey sat there trying to find the proper words.

"Good." The line went dead.

Lindsey put the phone down and turned to look out at the Bay. He shook his head and just wrote it off as a crank call, not believing that the next day the FedEx van would arrive with a cashier's check in the amount of $80,000 dollars. But it did. And with it were the instructions to send the papers to Dr. C. Thomas Mallory — as of now, a new resident of Clover Bay.

WAYNE E. HALEY

CHAPTER 3

The day was wet. The hot spell had finally ended and with it the cool fall rain started to fall on Clover Bay. Most of the folks in town were very happy that the thermometer had dropped to a reasonable 57 degrees. That was more like it, and the way things should be in Washington. These folks lived here because of what they called the "banana belt effect" caused by being in the rain shadow of the Olympic Peninsula across the Straits of Juan de Fuca. But calling something a banana belt and actually living in one are two completely different things.

About 9:30 A.M., a dark green 1950 Dodge station wagon came from the south end of town on Main Street — one of the only paved streets in Clover Bay. It had a chrome spotlight on the driver's door and a 102-inch whip antenna on the rear bumper. It had a triangular "Civil Defense" sticker on the passenger's side wind wing, and a small amber light in the rear window that made the car look like a block warden had formerly driven it. In small letters on each of the two doors were the words "FOR OFFICIAL USE ONLY." In fact, if you were living in 1950, the car would have looked very official. The only really unusual item about it was the fact that it gave off a strange subwoofer-type sound as it cruised toward Clyde Lindsey's office. A couple of people noticed that the car had Colorado plates. They also noted that the sound coming from it was something very much like an old 60s rock-and-roll sound, but all one could hear were the bass notes. As it pulled up in front of Clyde's office, the driver opened the door, filling the air with Tina Turner screaming about "Proud Mary." As the driver got out, he pushed the button on the Blaupunkt stereo and silence rushed in to fill the void. Doc Mallory had arrived in Clover Bay.

Dr. C. Thomas Mallory, Ph.D., D.D., N.D. was a total oxymoron, and when he stepped from the car it showed. He was a large man, over six feet. He was built like a bear with a salt-and-pepper beard and a full head of brown hair. He wore a tweed jacket with suede elbow patches. Under the jacket he had on a "Stanford" sweatshirt and brown bush pants. He sported a large curved briar pipe that he puffed on constantly, filling the air with noxious fumes. He stepped onto Clyde Lindsey's porch, and in that same moment the universe shuddered. It was a quick shudder, true, but still the universe knew — even if Clover Bay did not — that nothing would ever be quite the same.

Doc Mallory was a seeker of truth. He had spent his life in that quest. It was his grail. He had anointed himself and sallied forth to find truth wherever it was hiding. He believed in one thing — finding answers to questions for which people would say there were no answers. He had rarely believed them, not when he was young, and now, not at all. He had found the answers and he had made a decent living doing it.

As a young undergraduate, he had decided to live just as he desired. That had led him through a series of minor and major conflicts with college administrators, foundations, the governments of at least a half dozen countries and three ex-wives. He looked at all of these with reflection and disdain. They had not understood that within the three-pound universe of his brain, there lay the power to overcome any obstacle, including tenures in departments of psychology, anthropology, sociology, clinical medicine and parapsychology — all of which he had been fired from at one point or another in his career. He found if he could survive giving the opening lecture in any class that he was teaching, he might make it through the semester. But as any academician knows, department chairs have a way of finding out what goes on inside a closed classroom about as fast as the government or the phone company does. And that is quick to say the least.

But Mallory was a knight errant on his mission, most of which was to open and expand the consciousness of rather dull and completely servile students that just wanted an easy class and not a lot of homework. He would immediately launch into one of his famous diatribes about the nature of the universe, the meaning of life, the cause of the great depression, or why the story of Christ's crucifixion was a complete hoax dreamed up by four ne'er-do-wells that had nothing better to do than to screw up mankind for two thousand years.

Equally, outside the classroom, Mallory was always in hot water. At afternoon faculty functions, he would discuss the bust size among Hottentot bushwomen, and methods of destroying computer databases, especially those operated by credit bureaus and the U.S. Government. But his all-time favorite were methods of divination practices by shamans in the upper Amazon rain forest. He liked telling the story about being chased by a patrol craft while water skiing the Ganges in India during a cremation ceremony, or the night he got stoned and slept in the King's chamber of the Great Pyramid, or how he had been physically tossed out of a religious meeting for his own version of "talking in tongues" of which nobody had the slightest idea what he was doing.

He would goad other faculty members into raging disagreements, redirect their anger at a colleague and then slip out the side door leaving the room in bedlam. These actions always endeared him to the chair of the department. Normally about the third week, there would be a small note in his mailbox telling him that funding had been cut in the department (or that they had found the right person for "his" position), and that his services would no longer be needed. He would finish the term, give an "A" to everybody that didn't deserve it, a "F" to those that should have passed, and walk away completely screwing up the GPA of at least sixty students. He believed it was a small price to pay for the knowledge that he had willingly imparted to them.

He had done ETS, Eslen, Neurolinguistic Programming and Akido. He had been a vegetarian, a Hindu, a Buddhist, tried his hand at lay preaching, and generally worked only long enough to get enough money to carry him on one of his adventures to some distant and darkly lit corner of the globe.

He always took his portable computer, an old leather duffel bag that contained his change of clothes, and three boxes of relevant tomes for review and aid. This included books on medicine, psychology by Jung, Godel-Escher-Bach and Buckminster Fuller, and the complete works of Louis L'Amour — all of which fit into the Dodge station wagon that was now parked in front of Clyde Lindsey's office.

• • • • •

Lindsey sat at his desk thumbing through the papers that had accumulated over the past week. Nothing much of importance, only notices for public hearings, some questions about estate planning and the random inquiry as to whether one neighbor could sue another because their dog dug up the iris bed. He felt the wind from the open door and smelled a powerful smell reminiscent of a Greek Orthodox Church during Mass. There stood this man with a smoking pipe in his mouth and hand extended.

"Mallory here. You must be Lindsey." More a statement than a question.

"Yes, I am...aha." Lindsey wasn't sure if he should ask him to take the pipe outside or overlook it, since this man did represent, in one lump sum, the biggest amount of money he was going to earn for this year.

"Good. I can tell that you spent some time in India, have a small dog and use the Mahanadi brand of snuff imported by the East India Company." Mallory was studying the framed certificates and photos on the wall while he spoke.

"No, I haven't." Lindsey looked at the man with a puzzled expression on his face.

"Of course you did, in your last lifetime when you were a gentlemen of the Court of St. James. All these things are clear to one who knows the past, present and future." Mallory turned for the first time and stared at Lindsey. The latter went weak inside due to the stare.

"Did you know that 'if' is the middle word of 'life' and that 'aha' is the most common word in the English language? Watusis will go mad if you make them look at an object with a ninety-degree angle on it. And that one can not do a full spectrum analysis on laser light?" He puffed his pipe until it relit and smoke again emerged.

"Is all of this relevant to something?" Lindsey felt like an undergraduate trying to fathom the depth of the meaning of the diatribe and was slowly gaining a view that perhaps this man was a little over the edge, a couple of bubbles off true plumb.

"The questions forced you to think; suddenly 10 billion electrons flowed in your brain, and you think that I am goofy. Aha, but that is not the point. Where is the house, counselor? Let's see my estate." With that Mallory walked out of the office and started to walk toward the Dodge. Lindsey turned on his answering machine, fished his keys out of the left-hand desk drawer and locked the front office. Mallory turned and watched.

"You have a strong criminal element in these parts?"

"No! Why do you ask?" Lindsey found himself not liking this man at all, with his brusque manner.

"Then why lock the door?" Mallory pointed with the stem of his pipe. "Normally people secure things because they have a belief that someone is going to steal them. If you have no criminal element around here, then either you are exhibiting a great degree of paranoia, or you are someone who wants to keep secrets from his neighbors."

"Habit." Lindsey found himself trying to defend

a lifetime with one word.

Turning to enter the car, Mallory spoke over his shoulder to no one in general, "Need to think about what you do. If you are driven by habit, you could miss clearly a third of life as a waking human being. It is the Bardo, the time between being and not being that should concern you, Lindsey. If you read the *Tibetan Book of the Dead* you will gain insight into what it is that keeps you from the true success that you desire."

Before Lindsey could speak, Mallory was in the car and Tina Turner was filling the street again with Ike adding a simple "rollin" in the background.

CHAPTER 4

The house was seven miles out of town on a quiet country lane. The trees had started to turn their autumn colors, and leaves covered the edge of the road. As the Dodge rocketed down the lane, Lindsey found that he was both fascinated and repelled by this man. What had he meant by "the success you desire?" How could Mallory know nothing about him, and yet his words had struck a bell inside Lindsey's mind?

He pointed to the left or right in an effort to communicate because the music in the car was nearing the threshold of pain. Lindsey noticed that the dash had a collection of strange instruments, none of which were automotive. Various lights and gauges were moving and blinking in some rhythmic pattern, but their use alluded him. He finally pointed toward the driveway of the old house and the car came to an abrupt stop.

Mallory jumped out and started to pace the

grounds. He was holding a dowsing rod and stopping here and there, muttering. Lindsey walked up to him and asked as politely as he knew how, "Are you dowsing for water?"

"Hell no, there's water all around here. I'm trying to find zones of positive and negative energy, where they come and go through the latticework of the earth's crystallian grid. One cannot be too careful when it comes to noxious zones. Saw a man swallowed up by one in Burma years ago. Just reached up and sent him pan-dimensional — zap just like that. Hell of a way to go, wouldn't you say?" He walked off without waiting for a response.

"Pan-dimensional?" Lindsey wandered off behind Mallory and just fell into a silence that accompanies confronting the forces of good and evil, light and dark, or simply somebody who is nuts. Lindsey was formulating his next step. "Do you want to look at the inside of the house?"

"Nah, it's just a structure to keep the elements away. It is an outgrowth of caves and rock shelters. A little more refined, perhaps, but no real difference in purpose, you know. I prefer a house of rammed earth like the Jurgdi build in North Africa. But Jesus, by November here, those houses would fall apart and you'd have the worst case of arthritis you could image." Mallory pulled out a photometer from his pocket, pointed it toward the sun, and gave a shrug.

"Some folks around here say that the house should be placed on the National Registry of Historical

Structures due to the age and the distinct way that it was built — a traditional Northwestern architectural example of Benjamin Greer's style."

"It's a house, not a work of art, Lindsey. Priorities, people are always screwing them up." Mallory put the photometer away and relit his pipe. "But it's fine. Wouldn't change a thing."

Behind them a set of large flatbed trucks pulled up and a dark man in coveralls emerged. "I'm looking for Dr. Mallory."

"I'm Mallory; you must be from the Seattle Fencing Company?"

"Yup, what you need done?"

Mallory got into a long in-depth conversation with the man, pointing and waving his hands. The man responded with nods and shrugs and then walked back to his truck. Mallory returned to where Lindsey stood. "Okay, counselor, I'll drive you back to town now and get out of your hair."

"You know, we do have ordinances about fences and how they can be used in the county. They must conform to certain codes and...." Before he could finish, Mallory was back in the car and starting the engine.

"Rules are agreements to conventions only, Lindsey. They indicate our desire to protect the weak and promote a lack of courage. They serve only to enslave man, not liberate him. Jefferson was a true believer in the individual. He was the last one to sit in the White House that understood that man is a sacred

19

creature that uses his mind to overcome problems."
Mallory was driving at high speed back toward town.

CHAPTER 5

As the green Dodge pulled up in front of Clyde Lindsey's office, there was an air of confusion within the confines of the car. Lindsey was trying to determine the extent of the insanity that seemed to grasp Mallory, wrapping itself around him like an old plastic raincoat in a strong wind. Sensing this concern, Mallory turned toward Lindsey and pushed the "off" button on the radio. Silence filled the interior of the car except for the collective breathing of the two men.

"You know, Clyde, life is an ever-increasing circle, like the waves a pebble makes when thrown into the water. One cannot count the ripples that are produced by the single stone, yet each ripple is a complete and perfect circle, expanding into infinity. Within the range of human variations, there are thousands if not millions of types of individuals. We, you and I, are only two. Different and yet the same. As the bard said, 'If you prick us, do we not bleed? if you tickle us, do we not laugh...and if you wrong us, shall we not revenge?' Truly, all of life is a stage and we are but the players, Clyde, locked in this great comedy we call existence. You seek haven here in this backwater of reality. I seek a change, a new adventure. And before this act is over, you and I, and all the creatures that live in the confines of space and time, will have changed. For no system can come into action with another system and not be irrevocably changed by that meeting." With that, he lit his pipe and turned to face the street again. Lindsey sat there thinking about the words and what they meant.

"I will have some friends drop by from time to time, and I would appreciate it if you would give them directions to the house. Would you do that for me?" Without turning to look at the man, Mallory started the car again. Its engine murmured quietly.

"Sure, I would be glad to, but...." His words trailed off and ended in a myriad of garbled thoughts. He opened the car door, walked around the front and entered his office after unlocking the door. He stood in the early afternoon light, staring at the keys in his right hand. He did not hear the door open behind him, nor the footsteps that walked across the hardwood floor. He turned more by instinct than knowledge and studied the face looking at him.

"You okay, Mr. Lindsey?" The voice was detached from the body and it took a moment for Clyde to recognize it. It belonged to Deputy Bob Duncan, the resident deputy sheriff for this part of San

Juan County. He was a short, pudgy man with red cheeks and little pig-like eyes. Lindsey studied him for a moment; he looked at his shirt that pulled at the waist button and his gut that hung over his weapon belt.

"I'm fine." Lindsey felt extremely uncomfortable and slightly dizzy. "What can I do for you, Bob?"

"Nothing, I was just checking up on our *new* resident out at the old Twitchell house. What's he like? Seems like a real jerk in that getup and old car. Some kind of weirdo? Or do you think he's messed up in drugs, using or selling? Can't have that kind 'round here. What do you think?" Deputy Bob stood there with his short thumbs wrapped around his weapon belt, doing his best John Wayne or Chuck Norris impersonation.

"Jesus, Bob. He's a doctor. And what do you mean 'weirdo'? How could you ascertain all of that from seeing him drive into town. Bob, don't let your need to do something start you off on some wild goose chase. He's fine." Lindsey felt an irritation rising in him without knowing why. He had just defended a man who, not more than five minutes before, he had thought to be mad.

"Don't matter that he's a doctor. How about that one back in the sixties, Lear something? He was one, too, and started turning kids on to LSD and the like. And how about that one in Michigan that helps people to kill themselves? He's an M.D." Bob was convincing himself that he was right.

"I have work to do, Deputy. Thank you for your concern." The ceremonial dismissal was complete and final. Bob stood there for a moment and then turned and left without reply. He thought to himself about what he knew about Lindsey. He had only been here for three years. Maybe he was a weirdo, too. There would be a need to check on that as well. Couldn't be too careful. That was his job: protecting the *good* citizens of Clover Bay.

Lindsey walked back to his desk and sat staring out at the boats moored in the Harbor. They moved with the rhythmic motion of the ebb tide, swinging one way and then back the other. Mallory's word revolved in his head, over and over.

· · · · ·

Two weeks had passed. Clyde Lindsey was working on a couple of estate planning cases, a proposal to take before the county planning commission for Harv over at the barber shop to put up a new sign, and somebody had called him concerning a dog-bite case. They wondered whether they could sue for damages. As Mr. Lincoln had said, "Advice and time are a lawyer's stock in trade." He had not thought much about Mallory during this period — just an occasional random speculation about what the doctor was doing out at the old Twitchell place. But he had made an attempt to forget about the disturbing thoughts that came when he was with Mallory. He had told himself that he was content here at Clover Bay and that things were all right in his world.

He had not heard the black Citroen pull up outside his office, or the sound that its occupant made as she walked into the room. He first noticed her with his side vision and jerked his head up to look into blue-within-blue eyes, crystal blue, both pupil and iris. They were connected to a face that was cut from some amber piece of marble. She stood there, nearly six feet tall, with raven black hair and deeply tanned skin. A gold pendant hung between the exposed cleavage of her breasts. She wore a red silk blouse and black leather skirt, which exposed long tapered legs that ended in a pair of black patent leather, four-inch heels — not the average dress for a day on the Bay.

She had crossed her arms and a gold key chain with one key dangled from her wrist. She looked at Lindsey with a half smile and dancing eyes. They seemed to sparkle and twinkle like the night sky. The voice was low, soft and resonant. "You must be Clyde. I'm looking for Doc Mallory's place. He told me that you could show me where it is." The words were neither statement nor question.

He stood up and realized that she was a good three inches taller than he was. "Erh, well, yes, but...ah...." Lindsey pointed to his desk. "I have work that must get done and I, uh...." His voice trailed off as he looked into the pools of stars that were her eyes.

"More important than welcoming a visitor to

your quaint little town?" Her playful tone filled his mind. "Or, if you can just draw me a map, I am sure that I can find it."

"No! I mean no... I wouldn't think of it. The doctor wouldn't forgive me for being so, er...uh...uhm, vulgar." Lindsey fought to pull his eyes away from hers, but found the task harder than he had expected.

"You could not be vulgar, Mr. Lindsey, Plaxite on Gromax Seven are vulgar. However, half the galaxy knows that. Anyway, where can I find the good doctor?" She leaned on one leg and shifted her body position in a way that made Clyde a little weak inside.

"Oh, what the hell. This stuff can wait. I'll show you where he is. It's a little out of town, and I wouldn't want you to get lost getting out there." He fumbled getting his coat on and reached to open the door.

"Get lost? One would have a hard time getting lost here. Now in the Mydroxian star system people get lost. But that should be expected." She turned and walked out through the door, Lindsey close at her heels. She turned and looked back at the office.

"Aren't you going to lock the door?"

He stood for a moment and looked at her and the door and shrugged. "No, there is no reason to. There's no criminal element here in Clover Bay."

"Good." She stepped into the car and turned on the engine that made almost no noise at all.

As he sat down next to her, another realization came to him, "I didn't get your name."

"None was given. But it is The Royal Lady

Lydia of the Stygian Triangle, but that seems so formal. Just call me Lady Lydia, if you prefer." She started up the street with four or five of the local residents watching.

Harv at the barber shop scratched his bald head and turned to one of his customers. "Must be up from Seattle dressed like that. Couldn't be one of the local girls."

Paul Gridder, the local nurseryman, was in the barber chair watching also. "Don't recognize that car; must be one of those new Jap models. Nobody around here would own anything like that, I'm sure." Paul sat back for his weekly pleasure of having the long hairs around his neck shaved.

"Seattle, I reckon. Lots of strange folks down there. Heard anymore about the ferry service?" Harv went back to his barbering.

"No, but they say there is going to be a hearing on it in about four weeks. It wouldn't be a good thing if they discontinued service up here in the summer. A lot of tourist business would be lost. But that wouldn't affect you and me, Harv." The laugh was deep and robust.

"The hell you say." Harv turned and pressed down on the foam dispenser and the white lather erupted onto his hand. "If there are no tourists coming, then a lot of these folks around here aren't going to make it and they will move out. And we will end up owning white elephants in the middle of a dying town, for Christ's sakes."

"Hadn't thought of it that way." New thoughts were hard for Paul to deal with immediately. He would have to do some thinking on that for awhile.

"We'd better think about it, we had, 'cause if that ferry stops, this place is going to look like somebody just dropped the bomb, and I myself do not like the idea of moving back to Seattle or Tacoma to start all over again with less than five years till I can retire." The words hung in the air, lost to anyone but Paul, who was still ruminating on the first piece of new information. Paul's mind was approaching overload quickly. What about all those bulbs he ordered for next season already?

• • • • •

The road was still lined with fall colors. The broad leaves of the Canadian Maples were like old paper, yellow and orange, resting on the wet blacktop that led the way toward Mallory's.

The Citroen hummed down the road. Lindsey sat looking out the front window and not knowing what to say. Mydroxian system? He mused over this and wondered if this was one of Mallory's patients. If it was, maybe Clyde had entered the wrong profession.

A small white paw nudged his arm, and he looked down to see the yellow eyes of a large black cat with white paws looking up at him from the console between the seats.

"That's Haddoxes. He is a Navigator of the Guild." That statement lingered in the atmosphere of the car. Lindsey wasn't sure what he was supposed to do with it.

"Hi, Haddoxes." He ruffed the cat's fur and played with him for a moment. The cat seemed normal. Lindsey let himself look at the profile of the woman that was driving. He had spent most of his life in Los Angeles, and was used to seeing beautiful women, but this one was a work of art. Her features were chiseled and yet soft. The cat bit Clyde in a playful way. "Awa!"

"He likes you. Otherwise he would not play with you. Guild members are a strange type." She was turning the car onto Useless Bay Road when Clyde realized he was not giving her directions and yet she was driving straight toward the house.

"What do you mean *Guild members?*" Lindsey stopped his thought and pulled himself up as the car entered the driveway, now blocked by an eight-foot electrically operated gate.

A closed circuit television camera stared down at the car. A small gray box was mounted on a post on the driver's side. The post had a speaker and key pad on it. The gate was attached to a seven-foot chain link fence that ran completely around the property. He stared at the yellow sign attached to the gate:

WARNING!
YOU ARE IN A BIO-HAZARD ZONE.
DO NOT ENTER

"What's with the sign?" Lindsey spoke as if he expected Lady Lydia to understand or to know. It dawned on him that she had not been here before, so why should she know?

"One of Doc's little jokes to keep the neighbors away, I would imagine. He does things like that all the time. He is of the belief that those who would come beyond that kind of sign would have to be interesting enough for him to talk to. The rest he would not want to spend the time of day with." She lowered her window and pushed four buttons on the key pad and the gate jerked and started to open the portal.

"How did you know the code for the gate?" Clyde studied the side of her face.

"It is always the same. Push the numbers that correspond on a telephone keypad to spell O-P-E-N." She accelerated up the driveway and turned to watch the gate close behind them.

"There are ordinances, and normally one must get permission to put up that kind of gate, especially at a place that could be considered an historical monument." Lindsey found anger welling up inside him again. Every time he dealt with Dr. Mallory, he found that emotions long dormant came to the surface. He could not believe someone could be so insolent as to put up that kind of gate and fence around a place like this.

Mallory stood on the deck which ran around the house and was using a telescope to look across the Bay at something. He turned at the approaching noise of the car. He sauntered down the porch and walked to open the door on the driver's side. "The Royal Lady Lydia of the Stygian Triangle, I see."

She turned to Lindsey in the car. "He is always so formal in his address to royalty; it is a result of the high-priced education he has received. I have told him for years that it's okay to call me just Lady Lydia. But no, not Mallory. Playing to the audience all the time. Never a dull moment, I must confess." She lifted herself out of the car with a single graceful movement, and Lindsey sat there, transfixed again.

Mallory walked around to the rear of the car and pulled out the black leather traveling bag. He leaned down and studied Lindsey's face. "Going to stay in the car, or would you like to come up to the house, Mr. Lindsey?"

Lindsey sat still for another moment, drinking in the after-smell of her perfume. Then he came back to the moment. "Of course...ere, I would love to come in."

Mallory turned to Lady Lydia, who had again struck the pose of crossing her arms and leaning on one hip. "You still got that worthless piece of shit, Haddoxes with you. That no-account face-shifter from the other end of nowhere?"

From behind Lindsey, he heard the cat start to

hiss and spit and when he looked, the cat's ears where laid back and his fangs showed.

"Don't worry about him Lindsey. He is about as useful as tits on a boar hog." Mallory started to walk toward the house carrying Lady Lydia's bag. She leaned down and looked in at Lindsey, revealing more cleavage.

"Ignore the two of them. They just don't like each other a great deal and never have. It's an old struggle between them. It probably goes back to Bakas Revolt. Just ignore it." She smiled and walked along behind Mallory. Lindsey sat there for a moment and watched his world slowly pulsate in and out of reality. Shaking his head, he opened the car door and followed them up the path to the house.

· · · · ·

Lindsey had only been in the old house a half-dozen times, but he remembered its elegances and the tasteful way Margaret had it decorated. The scene that Clyde walked into was not what he had remembered. The drawing room was filled with equipment, buzzing and clicking away. The furniture was pushed to one side, and the oriental carpets were rolled up to form a barrier between the equipment and the disheveled furniture. Three small computers sat on a table under the window, and each had a different pattern of lines and shapes running across it. Mallory was coming down the stairs and walking past Haddoxes, who had just followed Lindsey into the house.

"Gerk Min Palxa," Mallory hissed back at the cat that spat and hissed and walked up the stairs. "Upstart little son-of-a-bitch. If I had my way, we would commit genocide through the galaxy on those little bastards." Mallory walked into the living room, pulled an office chair around from a desk, tossed himself into it, and lit his pipe.

"The cat?" Lindsey turned back to Mallory.

"Cat hell, those face-shifters can fool just about anyone, but that is no cat. The best of those scumbags make Nixon look like somebody you would invite to dinner and not check to see if he was stealing the silver service. And that little bastard is a far cry from the best of them. They are the slum lords of the universe. Watch him, Lindsey, he will steal your gold fillings should he get the chance." Mallory blew blue smoke into the air.

"I don't have any fillings." Lindsey mentally questioned the man that sat there. Insanity could not be contagious, could it?

"Well now, tell me about that place across the Bay where the old aviation control tower is." Mallory half pointed toward the scope on the deck outside.

"It was a Naval Aviation Training Center for years, but with the budget cutback and all, they closed it last year. They only use it now for summer drill for a couple of weeks for reservists. Why?"

Lindsey noticed the fish tank in the corner. It had a deep red tint to the water and three strange fish crawled around the bottom. He walked over to get a closer look. "Is there something wrong with your filter or something?"

"Just interested in it; don't like to be too close to the government. They claim that they're here to help, but in most cases that is not the truth. Nah, there is nothing wrong, the water is suppose to look like that. Especially to those types of fellows. Genetic hybrids, so to speak."

Lindsey didn't know a lot about fish, but he was sure he had never read anything about hybrids that lived in opalescent red water. "What is all this equipment for?"

"My work." Mallory was ruffling through some printouts from one of the computers.

"What kind of work?"

"Research."

"What kind of research?"

"Ray tracing and zone mapping of fluxation in the space-time continuum around the Zetta Epsilon Worm Hole, if you really need to know the truth. Now do you feel better with the answer?" Mallory seemed annoyed.

"No, I haven't the foggiest idea of what that is. Where is Lydia?" Lindsey turned toward the door leading to the staircase.

"For Christ's sake, Lindsey, never let her hear you call her that. A personal name address to her is 'Lady Lydia.' 'Lydia' by itself is the way a lover would address her. And in your case, not being initiated into that fraternity would bring on holy hell for you to deal with. Great God Almighty, is ignorance epidemic here?"

Lindsey turned back toward Mallory, still puffing away and typing something into one of the computers. "Is she a patient of yours?"

"I study her. Or we study each other for anomalies in perceptions. It's hard to explain in a few words exactly what it is all about, Lindsey." Mallory motioned to a chair for him to sit down.

"Where did all this equipment come from?" Lindsey was surveying the room again.

"Here and there, mostly shipped to me from storage." Mallory didn't look up to answer.

Lady Lydia walked into the room holding a silver tea service and placed it on a small corner table. She was wearing a black leather jumpsuit with zippers and a waist belt that only added to the stunning appearance of her body. The front zipper was pulled to mid-breast range and exposed the gold open triangle she wore about her neck. She wore a pair of jet black dress boots under the jumpsuit legs. "I needed to get comfortable and decided to make some refreshments for our guest," she indicated to Lindsey.

"Oh, yeah, forgot my manners again. Terribly sorry, old man," a response that seemed neither sincere nor appropriate to Lindsey, but he ignored it. He took the cup of tea that Lady Lydia offered, walked to the edge of the room and looked at the bookcase. Mixed up between *Godel-Escher-Bach* and a copy of *Lost Mesa* by L'Amour were four books. *The Bermuda Triangle Explained, Myth of the Space Gods, Inca's — The First Astronauts,* and *Haunting of Old Churches and Abbeys of England and Scotland,* on all of which the author's name was C. Thomas Mallory. "You wrote these, all of these?"

"No...I just had the jackets printed up to make it look like I did. Of course, I wrote them. They have been translated into fourteen languages and used as holy script among the less enlightened dwellers of this world. In the world of scholars there is but one rule: 'publish or perish.' But every time one of those books made it to print, a dean, provost, or chair of a department would walk into my office and stand there holding it and trying to compose the right litany of verse to tell me that this is not what the maxim of 'publish or perish' really meant." Mallory fumbled with his pipe cleaner and tapped the pipe on a large glass ashtray. "But they have given me a degree of freedom to continue my research and to be here." He waved at the surroundings.

"Ere...well...I need to be getting back." Lindsey stood there for a moment looking at both of them. "I could use a ride...." His voice trailed off as if he was requesting an unheard of thing from his host.

The voice was low and almost a whisper. "Take the Citroen, I won't be needing it for awhile."

"Oh...I couldn't think of...."

"Then walk." Mallory had turned to one of his

computers and Lindsey found himself staring again into those star-filled eyes.

"Take it, I'll pick it up later." She reached for his arm to escort him to the door.

Mallory raised a pipe-filled hand with his back to Lindsey, "Go with God, but go!"

At the front door he turned and looked at her again. "Ere...aha...." "Dinner, Friday, here at eight-thirty." She turned to look at Mallory's hunched figure as he dwarfed the machine he was pounding on. "Don't be late. He gets so annoyed when people are late."

"Sure, eight-thirty, Friday." Lindsey half turned back to her, "Can I bring anything?"

"Your mind, Mr. Lindsey. You seemed to have left it someplace along the long tunnel of time." She turned and walked back into the house without another word.

WAYNE E. HALEY

CHAPTER 6

Dixie Raye Russell had been in Clover Bay for seven years. The route she had taken was long, and oftentimes disappointing. But now she owned a little bit of her dream. Well, at least she and the First National Bank of Seattle owned a little bit of her dream. "Dixie's" was the only true restaurant in Clover Bay. It served breakfast, lunch and dinner, with cocktails as an added option. It was roomy and warm, with a lot of northwest ship memorabilia and pictures of great sailing ships from a bygone era on the walls.

The tourists that came to Clover Bay soon learned that "Dixie's" was the place to eat and drink, and to learn the history of the islands. And every year for four to five months, the place was filled with all sorts of naturalists, weekend adventurers, and just plain folks who wanted to get away from the hustle and bustle of the big city.

Dixie was thirty-five, blond and buxom, had a

peaches-and-cream complexion, and was in love with life. Since she was a little girl, she had dreamed of owning and running her own place. She had been the baton-twirling champion of Sand Creek, Idaho eighteen years previous to the now. She had gone onto the State Championships and had won a scholarship to the University of Idaho. In her sophomore year, she had fallen in love with a tailback on the varsity team. By her senior year she had married him.

Then one night, on a mud-slick field, he had tried a double-back, and was hit in the left knee by a 240-pound lineman. His knee was blown out completely, and so were his chances at the NFL and Monday Night Football. A few years of trying to find the right job made them gypsies, traveling throughout the northwest — he with another get-rich quick plan, and Dixie just wanting to settle somewhere and call it home.

They were traveling through Clover Bay when she looked at the old building that had been shut up for years and decided she had found her dream. There was a fight. He left and later sent her divorce papers from Alaska where he had found his pot-of-gold in the form of a travel agent in Fairbanks. They had planned to get married and have kids, and all the usual stuff that goes with newness and novelty of a fresh romance. Dixie had called her dad. Her dad co-signed at the bank for the mortgage, and Dixie signed the papers for the divorce and got on with her life. She had made a comfortable living in Clover Bay. Not great, but comfortable. And that was what she wanted.

She had been carefully following the happenings of the Seattle-to-Friday-Harbor Ferry, because that was her lifeline to the dream. Without it, there would be few tourists, and business from the locals was meager to say the least. Those five months in the summer and early fall were her time to make it for the year. And make it she had done for seven long years, 363 days of the year. She always closed on Christmas and her birthday.

So, it was understandable that she didn't notice the Harley-Davidson motorcycle pull up in front of the place and the single rider dismount. He was rough cut in his jeans and western shirt. He removed his helmet and replaced it with a Bailey Silverbelly beaver cowboy hat. He pulled a Zippo lighter from his shirt pocket, lit a Camel straight and walked into the restaurant. She was behind the bar reading the paper and not paying much attention. It was mid-afternoon and not many folks were around, since it was not lunchtime or dinnertime yet. He strolled up to the bar and sat on the barstool directly across from her. He put out his smoke in the glass ashtray and waited for her to look up. When she did, she stared into blue eyes, set into a tan face fringed with brown hair. Like a lion's mane, his beard was majestic. Their eyes met and she felt something inside, kind of like a main spring in a watch unraveling really quickly.

"You mess around on the first date?" Another Camel went to his lips, and the distinct sound of the

Zippo opening filled the space between them.

"Depends on who's asking," she folded the paper neatly and put it under the bar.

"I hear you serve whiskey here. That true? As to who's asking, I'm Ace." He took a long slow drag on his smoke and blew blue smoke up toward the open-beam ceiling.

She stuck her hand out to shake his. "Dixie Raye, and the answer is sometimes and yes."

"Sometimes you serve whiskey, and yes, you fool around on the first date, or visa versa?" His eyes danced with a glimmer that met hers in the space between them.

"Depends on what's more important right now to you, cowboy." She felt a warmth that she had not known in a long time. "Where you from, not around here, for sure."

"Well, that depends, also. Lately I've been in Peru, up the Urabamba River valley, flying supplies for a mining company. Before that, South Africa, flying mining supplies to a place out on the Rand that looked like God didn't even know it was there. But right now, Old Paint and me are here, and I'm thirsty." As he crushed out the smoke, she noticed the set of wings tattooed on the back on his hand.

"Old Paint? Somebody with you I didn't notice?" She looked around the bar.

"My horse out there, hitched to your post." He pointed with his thumb toward the window. She noticed the motorcycle for the first time.

"The Harley. Your horse?"

"Little faster than Old Paint, but still a bronc by nature." He gave her his biggest "go-ahead-and-trust-me" smile.

She reached back and pulled down a bottle of Jack Daniels and poured a measure and a half in the glass and put it on the bar. "Every cowboy I have ever met only drinks this. Am I right?"

He picked up the glass and drained it in one long shallow. "Yup, you sure know your cowboys, ma'am. Now, what time does the owner let you free from this place, and where can we go and have some fun? Do a little two step and howl at the moon."

"Slow down, cowboy. I am the owner, and this is the place where people dance and howl at the moon in Clover Bay. I am not sure a lady like myself should be seen cavorting with a drifter like you, Ace." She filled his glass again, and this time he just sipped at it.

"Eureka, I found me a woman of substance," he announced as if to the world and looked around. "Not exactly doing a land office business right now, are you?"

"It's almost the end of the season, and things are a little slow with the economy and all. But it picks up about suppertime, and a lot of the people on day hikes come in to have a warm meal and lie to each other about how far into the forest they walked and what they saw."

She walked around the bar and sat down next to him and turned to look at him. "What brings somebody like you up here to the end of nowhere?"

He drained his glass and turned to her. "An old war buddy got him a spread around here. Going to visit for awhile. Could extend my visit if the likes of you were inclined to visit a spell and tell me your life history, Dixie."

"Not a lot of interesting material there, cowboy. Just a hash-slinger that's never been farther east than Lewistown, Idaho or farther south than Portland, Oregon. Not a world traveler like yourself." She turned to where her knees were touching his thigh.

"Ain't missed much, I can tell you that. Most towns look the same, and most people are the same. Just folks trying to get by and see that their children are fed and that they have a warm place to live and sleep." He pulled another Camel out and lit it. "But you know that. That's why you put down a taproot here and plan to hang on and stay."

"You think so?" She played with him in a defensive sort of way.

"You bet. Folks like you are settlers. They made this country and most others just by doing what you are doing. Open a little business and work hard at it, and after awhile they make it. The only real problem is knowing what the *it* is that they want to make. Some folks are looking to get rich, some want fame and the fortune that goes with that, but some are more realistic and just want to know that if tomorrow comes they will be ready to meet it on their own terms; and if it doesn't, then it won't matter to them."

"Philosopher and cowboy. Quite a combination, Ace. I close at ten, need to clean up and willing to have 'a' drink with you. See how it goes from there, deal?" She smiled at him and showed a prefect set of pearl white teeth that reflected a truly good heart and soul.

"Okay, fine by me. I'll be here at ten to help clean up." He dropped a five on the bar, "and have 'a' drink with the pretty lady."

"Who's the friend you're looking for, by the way? Maybe I know him."

"Doc Mallory, the worst piece of human flesh God ever made. But a friend and partner for twenty years."

"Well, that figures. He's been here a month and he's the talk of the town. Bought the old Twitchell place around the other side of the Bay. Put up a hurricane fence and electric gate. Just made everybody around here crazy with curiosity. He comes in once or twice a week to have dinner. Has a beautiful and strange woman with him. But that's none of my concern. Small towns talk just because they have nothing better to do with their time. They say he is some kind of scientist. Is that right?"

"Boy howdy is he — probably the brightest man I ever met, and down to earth when you know him well." Ace pulled away from the bar and pointed to three directions of the compass.

"Take the main street to Useless Bay Road.

Follow it north to Twitchell Road, and then about three more miles on the left. You won't miss it; it looks like a federal prison with all that fence around it." She got up and walked behind the bar. The question hung in the air, unspoken. He walked toward the door and turned.

"Ten, and don't be late." He walked out without another word.

She started to wipe down the bar and broke into laughter. Talking to nobody but the room, "Jesus, Dixie. A quick smile, and you said "yes." And a flying cowboy to boot. The worst of all worlds. Girl, you've gone over the edge."

CHAPTER 7

Deputy Bob had been paying close attention to the Mallory place. He had photographed it from each side through the foliage. He'd had the photos enlarged and had pinned them onto the corkboard in his office. With a red marker, he had circled those areas that looked suspicious to him and had started to keep a daily report of activities — the comings and goings at the place. He had noted that the new occupant, a woman, looked foreign. Might be Colombian or Venezuelan. He had noted the times when delivery vehicles showed up, and the kind of equipment that they took off the trucks and loaded into the house. He especially watched Mallory's comings and goings. After a month, Deputy Bob was convinced that Lindsey, the outsider from L.A. who had only been in Clover Bay for five years, was Mallory's contact. He was sure of it. But he would need more manpower if he was going to maintain a proper surveillance of these people and find out just what was going on.

He loaded up the patrol car with his photos, daily reports, and other information to make his case and drove to the main office in Anacortes. He knew the boss would be proud of him for breaking this big a case.

CHAPTER 8

Deputy Bob's life was not going well. He had not had that kind of ass-chewing since he was a rookie just out of the academy. But it seemed like the boss did not like his idea that something was amiss out at the old Twitchell house. And the boss had made that point really clear to him. He had listened carefully and looked at the dimly lit pictures of an old house with a large chain-link fence around it. He had listened to how Deputy Bob had spent dozens of man-hours in surveillance, and then he finally exploded. It was sort of like Hiroshima all over again.

Bob didn't know that somebody could actually swear for forty-five minutes and never use the same words twice, but he had learned that it could be done. He didn't think the Sheriff was right about his family tree being a straight line, but then again, Bob wasn't quite sure what that meant either. He did understand though, that this case was not a case, and he would not, repeat, would not spend one more minute on it under any circumstances. Bob put his pictures, his reports, and his opinions into his brief case and headed back toward Clover Bay. He knew that the best possible thing to do was to vanish for maybe four to six months and only answer those radio calls that were absolutely necessary. He believed he was right, but when it came to paychecks, there was no arguing with the boss. So, whatever crimes were being committed at the old Twitchell house would just continue right on without his attention.

Now he had to go and talk to old man Morton. The old geek lived by himself out on Useless Bay Road, about a mile from the Twitchell house, and had called to report that something or someone had killed two of his best sheep.

"Best sheep, my ass," Bob grumbled under his breath as he drove down Useless Bay Road. "Probably they were his answer to old miss rosy four fingers."

He did not like Morton. He had always thought him strange, living out there alone with a dozen sheep in his yard. Bob had heard all the jokes in town about sheep herders and laughed with the boys at the bar over them. In fact, he could easily believe the jokes applied to old man Morton. "Probably killed one in the heat of passion."

He pulled up in front of the little house and put on his best "I-am-the-law-and-I'm-here-to-help-you" look.

"Good Day, Mr. Morton. I got a report from

dispatch that you wanted to see a deputy."

"Sure, two frinking hours ago I wanted to see you...but no — probably had more important business than rustlers." The old man was leaning on a shovel in the front yard.

"Got out here as soon as I could, sir." Deputy Bob stepped inside the white picket fence gate and, holding his clipboard, looked around. "What's all this about rustlers?"

"Two of my sheep are gone." The man spat a blackish clump of chew from the corner of his mouth. "Look over there and see what you make of it, young fellow."

Bob walked over to the pen that held the other sheep. He looked around, but didn't see anything out of the ordinary. "What exactly am I looking for, Mr. Morton?"

"That's it. You look but don't see. Two sheep are gone. Count them. There are nine. There used to be eleven. Now there are nine. That means that two are missing." Morton grumbled something under his breath.

"What was that, sir?"

"Nothing." The old man walked away still grumbling.

Bob took out his notepad and wrote that two sheep were supposed missing from the sheep pen at... (he had to think of what the old man's first name was — Hiram)...Hiram Morton's place on Useless Bay Road. "Could be Indians down from the reservation on Long's Island looking for a little mutton roast."

"Nah, the dog would have ate them alive."

"What dog?" Bob suddenly found that his entrails had started to grow warm and loose. A dog that would eat Indians probably would like sheriffs too.

"That dog, Blue. Had him for years. Tears the hell out of anything that walks in the yard," the old man was pointing at the woodpile next to the house.

Visions of shredded flesh flashed in front of Bob's mind. He looked around for Cujo. His gaze finally fell on a large Collie laying by the woodpile shaking and whimpering.

"He doesn't look...aggressive." Bob didn't move.

"Not now. But normally you'd not have gotten through that gate." The old man walked over to him and looked down. "But something scared the crap out of him. He hasn't moved for at least three hours."

The old man walked back to the Deputy. "Now, what the hell are you going to do about it?"

"I'll file a report and start an investigation right away." He nodded, made it to the gate, and when he got to the other side, he gave a small sigh of relief.

"A report. An investigation. For pity's sakes what about my sheep?"

"I will be getting back to you about them as soon as I know something more." Bob got back into the car and started down Useless Bay Road. Wonderful. A major syndicate going up at the Twitchell house, and now he was taking reports on missing sheep and scared dogs. He was glad, however, to be back in the protective womb of the patrol car. He wondered if the dog had eaten something to make it sick. It took about two miles and three minutes before he had completely forgotten about the missing sheep. He mentally dismissed them to the hands of some Indians that had tired of eating smoked salmon.

WAYNE E. HALEY

CHAPTER 9

As the electric gate slid open, Ace drove his motorcycle up to the front porch and parked it. Mallory stood there looking down at him. "How the hell did you find me? I figured I covered my tracks well enough that you couldn't find me this time."

"Luck of the draw, pard. Called Lady Lydia, and she told me that you were up here trying to prove another one of those weird theories of yours." He stepped up onto the porch and looked out around the Bay. "Nice place. You haven't completely hidden the view with antennas, parabolics, or the like yet."

"I'm working on it. The water gives a great reflective backplane for transmitting signals into the ionosphere. Anyway, what's up and why are you here?" Mallory packed his pipe with a fresh load of tobacco. His eyes never rested on any one spot. They were always moving, searching, and probing — a habit he had learned that made most people extremely uncomfortable. Most, but not Ace.

He pulled a Camel from his silver case, lit it with his Zippo lighter, and blew a cloud of smoke up into the air, watching as it drifted toward the Bay. "Needed a rest. Been doing a lot of flying lately and wanted a couple of good meals, a place to lay my head, probably some strange conversation, and your company."

"Hogwash!" Mallory exploded. "You're broke, out of a job, running from another charge by the law in some god awful South American country, or your ex-wife found out you got paid and has her lawyers after you again."

"Yeah, that too, but what the hell."

Suddenly, both men threw their arms around each other and slapped the other on the back in true friendship. Mallory held Ace by both arms and looked at him hard. "Jesus, I thought they had killed you for sure this time, you crazy bastard."

"Close, but no cigar. But...." He walked over to his motorcycle, opened one of the side bags, pulled two bundles from it and handed them to Mallory. "Those," he nodded toward the bundles, "are why they wanted to stand me in front of a wall, pray some vespers over me, and drill a half a dozen seven point six five millimeters through me. But they didn't and those are yours."

"What are they? Well, I...." Mallory was fumbling between the packages and his pipe. "They are...er...."

"Does this place have any rooms in it, or just a porch?" Ace was walking toward the door.

"Of course, go in...please." He was studying the wrappings that looked to him to be a hemp or palm leaf of some kind.

Ace walked into the converted living room and sized up the equipment and the computers. "You got fired again, right? So it's back to work on the project..." he paused, "...the time project?"

"Yes...." Mallory was slowly unwrapping the packages on the old Chippendale table.

Lady Lydia walked into the room in her black jumpsuit. She looked Ace up and down in a long slow stare. "Hi...."

"The Royal Lady Lydia of the Stygian Triangle." His voice was musical as he said it. "God — you just keep getting prettier and prettier."

"Charm. You are such a smooth creature, Ace. How have you been since the last time I saw you?" She sank into one of the overstuffed chairs.

"'Bout the same, running and gunning for God and Country." Ace was smiling his best "you-can-believe-anything-I-say" smile.

"Of which you believe in neither." She was watching Mallory fuss with the wrappings on the packages. He was studying them with a magnifying glass.

Feigning pain, Ace held his hand over his heart. "I'm shocked to say the least. Me, a patriot and all."

"Your loyalty lies with money, Jack Daniels, and this reprobate of a partner of yours. If this world had a decent religion, each of you would have been tied to a post and put to the flames years ago."

"Cold hearted. That, ma'am, is what you are," he still smiled.

"You and I both know that very well, but that is a physiological fact as opposed to a sentimental feeling."

"Great Caesar's Ghost, where in the hell did you get these?" Mallory was holding up a pair of black earthen pots with the same respect one would expect from the knights upon finding the Grail.

"I crashed in the jungle in the Antasoya of Peru. Plane shot to hell by rebels, copilot dead before we hit the ground, and no place to go but into the tops of those trees." Ace pulled a hip flask from the left side of his vest and took a long pull, wiping his mouth with the back of his hand. He turned and extended the flask to Lady Lydia. She had a half smile on her face and shook her head. He shrugged and replaced the hip flask in his inside vest pocket.

"You always were hard on copilots." Mallory was closely inspecting the urns with his magnifying glass.

"The place was pretty hot, so I figured it was time to vamoose my ass out of there. Made it about four clicks down-river. Then I found this cave. It seemed to be a fine place to hole up for a night or two until the unfriendlies would figure I was dead, snake bit, or in some tribe's pot for dinner. Ended up spending three nights in there 'cause I found a ceremonial altar in the back of the cave. It looked more

Chimu than Incan. Started to dig around and found those. Bingo! Look on the side." He pointed to a clear set of markings that stood out under the glass. "Those, Doctor, are ciphers of some kind."

"Couldn't be. Chimu and Inca did not have written language; used knotted ropes to communicate, a numerical-based language." Mallory was fully absorbed in the images on the pottery.

"Yeah, well, you tell me those don't have a look to them of cyclic repetitiveness." Ace pointed.

"Oh, dear." Lady Lydia was smiling. "The scholar can emerge on demand, and the West Texas drawl diminishes."

"Whoops," Ace looked back at her. Both smiled and then broke into laughter.

"Hungry?"

"Could eat a steer."

"How about a sandwich and glass of milk?"

"Sounds good to me. By the way, where is Haddoxes?"

"He'll be along. He's out looking around the neighborhood for some entertainment, I would believe." She walked toward the back of the house.

"Oh, boy. Haddoxes's idea of entertainment may not go over real well up here, Your Ladyship." Ace followed her.

"Life is sometimes that way."

They left Mallory sputtering and writing down symbols from the two urns. He would ejaculate a laugh mixed with a sound of exasperation. Puffing his pipe, he held the urns out at arm's length, taking in their own particular beauty.

CHAPTER 10

The night was wet. The fog had rolled in and was hanging like a shroud over Clover Bay. Droplets the size of goose eggs fell from the three lamps that illuminated the main street, splashing as they hit the sidewalk. The gray clouds lay so close to the ground that they seemed like living beings trying to find every nook and crevice to crawl into. The town was still. The lights in most of the shops and buildings along Main Street were dark. The only light visible came from the diner — a small glow that struggled into four feet of fog and was smothered by the heavy sea-laden air.

Dixie Raye and Ace sat at a small table in the corner, a bottle of Jack Daniels between them. Her hair was down covering her shoulders, and her feet were propped up in the cowboy-cum-aviator's lap, being massaged slowly. "...Well, that's about it. That is how I got here and what it is that scares me so much.

If that ferry stops running, this place is not going to make the mortgage payment, let alone enough for me to live on. Sad story, eh...?"

She looked across at a man that had been a stranger that very afternoon, and now seemed like her only real friend in the world. She had noticed that his harsh abrasiveness had fallen away, and a gentle soul had shown itself. "You're not like other men, Ace..." she started.

He held up a hand in protest. "Sure I am, just like the rest."

"No, you get to know people. Serving food, listening to their bad jokes and laughing when you think they're disgusting. All the guys that come in here from Seattle and Tacoma, they see a waitress and they figure they are away from the wife or girlfriend. What the hell. Maybe she'll fall for a good line, a quick roll in the hay, a shy good-bye, and off to the ferry dock — another notch in their belt." She sipped her drink. "But you haven't even made a bad joke or tried to look down my blouse. And here I am, feet up in your crotch, half pie-eyed, wanting you more than I think you want me and you are still a perfect gentlemen."

"Don't mean I ain't interested, Dixie Raye Russell. Just means that you're tired, a little lonely, and had 'a' drink with a friend. But come around sun up, I don't want no woman looking at me like something that ought to be killed, drug out the back door, and buried before the morning's half over." He pulled a Camel from his shirt pocket, set it on the table and stared at it for awhile. "Man like me don't look back much. Not healthy. I've been traveling from place to place for more than twenty years looking for something that I don't believe exists. But, still I look. This is the first time in a long time I slowed down long enough to pay much attention." He lit the cigarette and sipped at his drink. "But when you ain't tired and had 'a' drink, you make me the same offer and I'll show you how interested I am."

"You're something else, Ace." She put her feet down and leaned across the table. "How long you and the Doc been friends?"

"About twenty two years, give or take one." He reached across and held her hands, looking at them. His touch was soft and smooth.

"Tell me about it, cowboy?" She felt his fingers work into the grooves between hers.

"Oh, it's a long story and not real interesting." He let go and walked over to the jukebox. He dropped a quarter into it and played an old song, slow and kinda melancholy.

"You got someplace better to be tonight or somebody more willing to listen?" She sat back and ran her hand through her hair.

"Can't say that I do, but you will probably be bored to tears." He sat back down and filled her glass and then his.

"Try me."

"Okay. But remember, you asked for it." He crushed out his smoke and looked back into that dim past that so often seems to be a blur to most people. "The place really don't matter much, but it was down in Southeast Asia. A war was going on that nobody really cared much about except those that were trying to stay alive and go home. I was a fresh faced kid, just out of college and looking for adventure. I hired on with Air America, a bunch of spooks that were flying junk all over Asia and trying to make people believe that it was for some patriotic reason. After about eight months of this, getting shot at and crashing in the middle of nowhere, I wasn't a fresh faced kid anymore, but more like a bitter guy that thought life sucked. Then there was this mission that nobody wanted to take.

"There was a mission station run by a bunch of priests and nuns up-country in Laos. They had their hands full taking care of civilians that were in the wrong place at the wrong time; and a bunch of kids, orphaned by the stupidity of men, that wanted to place some other colored flag over a village that somebody else wanted their colors flying over. Most of these folks couldn't have cared less whose flag was up the pole, as long as they could raise their crops, feed their kids, and keep from getting killed by guys on either side of right or wrong." His eyes looked deeply into hers and she was almost transfixed listening.

"Go on, Ace...please." She reached out and touched his hand.

"Well...everybody that knew anything figured that this mission station was a goner. Nobody was going to fly in and try to get those folks out. Most people that watch movies or television think they know what that would be like. But that is all just horse manure. People dying is real. It is not a movie that you can rewind when you're done and send it back to the video store and say Gee, that was fun; let's get another and watch some more senseless killing, raping and violence and let's order a pizza. Nope. It's awful. So, I asked around to see if anybody would fly up there with me to pull those folks out. I didn't have a good reputation for keeping copilots alive. I had lost three of 'em in eight months. So, most of 'em were a little squeamish at the thought of, one, flying with me, and, two, going on what everybody said was a one-way flight. 'Too hot,' they said. 'Never make it in and out.' Nope. Nobody."

He lit another smoke and walked over and stared down into the workings of the jukebox. He rolled in another quarter and pushed another set of buttons. "Well, this big guy walks up to me. Beard, pipe jammed in his mouth, crazy eyes never staying still. He looks at me and says 'You going into Peh Wak?' I nod. 'Nobody going with you to help?' I nod again. He says 'I'll go.'

"You're nuts buddy, was my reply. He looks at me and hands me a card. It says *C. Thomas Mallory, Ph.D.*, that's all. I asked him if he was some kind of spook working for the Agency. He told me he'd just come to take a look.

"Well, the long and short of it is that he had

been in-country for six months. He had a grant from some agency that had six or eight initials instead of a name. It was given to study people's reactions under hazardous conditions. I asked him if he could fly, and he looked right at me and said 'no.' So I figure this guy is gone around the bend. It happens in the bush. Too long without human contact and in the middle of a war zone people just go crazy. But this guy has brass balls the size of basketballs. Nobody is going in; these folks are going to die up there and this guy is not even working up a sweat. I look around for other volunteers, none of which are to be found. And I look back at this nut who is sitting on a duffel bag, reading a copy of Kipling's Poems." Ace came back to the table and moved his chair close to hers and put his arm around her shoulders and let her lean her head on his shoulder.

"Well, twenty minutes later he and me and the C-123 were in the air. Mallory is talking to me about space-time continuums, warps in space, his theory of why the Anasazi disappeared, who the Mayans were in reality, and acting like nothing was going on except a flight from LAX to SFO.

"I'm pointing to smoke on the ground about five clicks from the landing strip, which was at the station. He puffs his pipe, looks out through the windscreen and pulls up his duffel bag. Inside, he's got two automatic pistols and a short barrel shotgun. Loads the works up, unbelts himself and is in back lowering the landing platform before I'm on final approach. He comes back up to the flight deck and yells in my ear,

'Just keep this son-of-a-bitch running and I'll take care of the rest.' I had no idea what that meant at all. So I drop her in and get her turned back into the wind. He hits the ground running, yelling in French, Laotian, and Vietnamese, and swearing at priests and nuns in some Chinese dialect that nobody has used for two hundred years.

"Boom! Then another boom! Holy shit, the airstrip is starting to disappear into bits and pieces. I yell that we have to go. 'Oh no, not yet.' He's loaded forty people, six nuns, two priests and a half a dozen goats and pigs in the back of the bird. He comes running across the strip with a box. For God's sake, what could be that important? I start to accelerate the bird. It's time to go.

"Then, out of nowhere, a round goes right through the outside skin of the plane and lodges itself in my left leg. Screwed to the wall, let me tell you, Dixie, darling. My whole miserable life passed in front of my eyes. Sadly, it was in black and white and not really very interesting. I'm bleeding like the proverbial stuck pig and there is no way I can manage to fly and bleed to death at the same time.

"So, here we were all wrapped up in this tin coffin waiting for the bad guys to come and get us. Suddenly, there he is looking down at me. He puts a rope around the top of my thigh and stops the bleeding. He looks at the strip that is now half as long as it was two minutes before, then looks back into the cabin space. He jumps into the copilot's seat and says, 'We can't leave them here; those bastards won't know what to do with them. They'll probably use them for toilet paper.' By this time I know I am in shock. He isn't making any sense to me at all. Then he looks down the ramp, lights his pipe, pushes the big black knobs straight to the fire wall and we start to roll right at a hole in the runway big enough to hide the Queen Mary. Gone for sure — the only thought in my mind. Then we are thirty meters from the hole with nothing for air speed, and he hits the right brake and rudder. The plane starts to spin around. People in back are screaming and yelling. He pushes the throttles again all the way and it starts to roll. By this time I'm poleaxed. I'm yelling at him over the engine roar, You can't make a downwind take off with this much weight. 'Nonsense,' he says, 'the plane doesn't know which way the wind is blowing.' But it's physics, it can't be done, I say. 'Bullshit. Don't believe them,' and he launches into a discussion about Simon Newcomb lecturing the American Academy of Science about how heavier than air crafts could never fly, the same day that two bicycle mechanics are out at Kitty Hawk with string and paper.

"This is not made of string and paper, I tell him. 'Exactly,' he shouts and pushes the beast until it's rattling like it's going to come apart at the seams. And suddenly, we are over the tree line screaming south. To say the least, I am a little annoyed. You said you didn't know how to fly — 'I didn't,' he says, 'but I watched you.' You watched me? — 'Exactly. Didn't seem that difficult.'

"An hour and half later we are unloading people at a friendly airstrip in Thailand and they are rushing me off to the hospital. Before they hauled my ass off, I grab him by the sleeve and ask him what he meant by 'they would use them for toilet paper.' He holds up some old yellow books from the box he had loaded last into the airplane. *The works of Dr. Erick Schulman, M.D.* — 'his diaries from forty years working with native plants in the highlands. Priceless.'

"I pass out and the next time I see him is in Boston. He is teaching at a college and I sit in on one of his lectures. Three years later, after putting up with endless amounts of bullshit and badgering from him, I get a Ph.D. in Psychology and know a hell of a lot more about flying than I ever did sitting in a cockpit."

"And you two have been friends ever since?" She picked up the bottle, placed it back behind the bar and put the two glasses in the sink.

"Yeah, well we keep finding each other and for some strange reason it has always held together." He picked up his smokes and put them in his pocket.

"If you want breakfast, I'm going to need some sleep, so you can either call me or nudge me, Ace." She stood in the doorway that led to the stairs that went up to her living quarters.

"Well this old cowboy needs to blow the cobwebs out. Me and Old Paint are going to take a spin around the Bay. But, kind lady, how about a rain check?" He walked over and gave her a long, deep kiss.

"You know where I am when you want to call in that rain check."

He let himself out, pulled up the collar on his flight jacket, tested the wind with his finger, and kicked the motorcycle into life. He liked her — a lot.

CHAPTER 11

Tishero Omishi Meshutoma was the eldest son of the Meshutoma Clan in Kyoto, Japan. He had been given a transistor radio for his sixth birthday. He had taken it apart with one pair of needle-nose pliers and a small jeweler's screwdriver. He wanted to know how it worked and why. The surprising thing was that he got it back together and it still worked. NHK, the Japanese Broadcasting Company, still came in and the one-and one-half-inch speaker still played the haunting melody of the floor harp. Tishero's life had been formed. He wanted to know why and how electrons worked and what it took to build things electronic. His father was only slightly pleased, since Tishero had one great drawback. He was mute from birth. His father knew that he could never go through the University of Tokyo because of the shouting requirement that all the new generations of captains of industry were required to have before graduation.

Tishero would neither be the head of a great electronics firm, nor even a middle manager, for those positions required speech. But his father fostered the boy's love for electronics with various kits bought from around the world.

Tishero would build and rebuild the kits, improving on their design. When his time came to go to college, Tishero opted to go to MIT in Boston and study electrical engineering. Like most Asian students, he caused the bell curve in the class to skew to the right because he was a 4.0 scholar in every class that he took. He had decided to spend his life in microprocessor research and stick to the lab where words would not come between him and his work.

He went to Stanford in Palo Alto, California for his master's degree. This was his undoing. He was bored one night with studying and listening to his stereo, so he decided to take in a lecture at one of the small community colleges in the area. The subject was U.F.O.s, "Visitors or Illusions?" The professor that was speaking was one C. Thomas Mallory, Ph.D.

Tishero sat in the front row of the tiered lecture hall transfixed for an hour-and-a-half, while this wild man paced back and forth, gesticulating and pontificating about what it would take to make an electrical spacecraft work. Some of the theory was outstanding and quantum in nature, and some was so far-fetched that Tishero laughed inwardly. At one of his silent guffaws, the bearded speaker looked directly at him for 30 seconds. It seemed to Tishero like an eternity.

He had spent the last twenty years trying not to have people look at him. Then in fluent Japanese sign language, Mallory asked him if he had a problem with what was being said. Tishero, amazed that the man could sign — and in Japanese — replied yes, and why? At this juncture, Mallory started to fill the whiteboards with equations concerning Magnetohydrodynamics. At one point, he tossed Tishero a marker and pointed to the board. Tishero went up to it, started to finish the equation, and then added some items that caught Mallory completely off guard.

After ten minutes of a heated exchange in sign, Mallory turned to the audience and told them the lecture was over, to the grumbling dismay of many. But as most straggled out of the room, discussing the strange man and the even stranger diatribe he had presented, a few hung around. Then as they slowly perceived the lecturer was going to ignore their comments, they, too, left.

Two hours later, when the custodians came into the quiet room, they found two men standing at the front of the room rapidly signing to one another and throwing down ink markers. One of the men was ejaculating groans and mumbling the nameless names of God under his breath. The other was pounding his hands together at high speed, only to have the larger man respond at an equally high speed. One of the custodians innocently asked, "Are you both dumb?"

"Do we look like we're dumb? Can you figure out this damn equation?"

"You can talk?"

"Jesus, Mary, and Joseph, of course I can talk. So what?"

"Then why are you speaking to the Chink in sign language?"

"Oh, for the love of mercy. He's not a Chink, you dumb bastard. And it's because it's easier to communicate in the language in which he thinks, which is Japanese; and it's easier for me to do that in sign than it is in his own language. What the hell do you want?"

"We need to clean up the room and erase the whiteboards." The custodian did not leave the back of the room. He was not sure if he wanted to get too close to what was going on.

"You touch those boards and I will break your goddamn neck." Mallory turned and continued his silent conversation with Tishero.

"Look, Buddy, I'm going to call security and they will have your ass and this Chink slope out of here in about two minutes. So...."

Suddenly Mallory started to walk up the tiered room step by step, and as he went his voice started out low and menacing. "You can call security, you can call the police, you can call the FBI... you can even call Dr. Harvey, the College President. And you tell him that his old buddy, Dr. Mallory, wants to use this classroom for the next two days over the weekend. But if you touch the work on any of those boards, your widow will retire at Club Med and find a twenty-year-old stud, and everybody will say...," he poked at the custodian's nametag on his white uniform, "...what ever happened to old Bill? You know why? 'Cause they wouldn't be able to recognize you even from the dental records. Now, go call Dr. Harvey and find out if I am right — jerk." Mallory loomed over the man. Tishero was filling one of the other whiteboards with more equations. The custodians left and Mallory returned to the platform at the front of the room and lit his pipe. He watched for three more minutes and then started to laugh. Tishero turned and looked at him and started to sign very quickly.

"My mother never did, you little bastard." He grabbed the marker and wrote three equations in his precise script. Tishero stood there looking amazed. He walked back and started to follow the linear progression of the equations when a security guard came in and stood at the top of the stairs. "Dr. Mallory?"

"Yeah, what?"

"Dr. Harvey said it was fine that you use the classroom for the weekend. He just said, 'don't burn it down or blow it up.'"

"Fine, now get out and lock the damn door. I've had enough interruptions for one evening." Mallory's eyes never left the small oriental working his way through the equations point by point. He reached the fourth board, turned and looked at Mallory with total disbelief in his eyes. Then he pointed to the last equations and pounded his fist on the board, shaking his head from side to side. Mallory walked over to the old duffel bag on the floor. He pulled out a plastic-wrapped tuna sandwich. He opened it, smelled it, and handed half to Tishero. Without looking, Tishero started to eat it. Mallory next pulled a bottle of scotch from the bag, took a swig, and handed it to Tishero who did likewise. Then he pulled out an old beaten up copy of Tesla's *Invention, Lectures and Research*, opened it to a section that was highlighted in yellow, green, and red. He pointed to a paragraph and handed it to Tishero.

Tishero was holding a book in one hand, the bottle of scotch in the other, and half of a tuna sandwich in his mouth. He chomped down and finished the sandwich, took two more long swigs from the bottle, and handed it back to Mallory. Tishero walked to the board and studied the equations. He read and then reread the highlighted section of the book, turning the pages rapidly and reading each section quickly. Suddenly he looked up at the board and used the eraser on a section of the equation he had written. He replaced it with another equation completely and then restudied the book and looked at the last three equations Mallory had put on the board.

He walked past Mallory, took the bottle out of his hand and sat down in the front row. He looked from the very first equation to the last and repeated the process four times; each time he would finish the pass with a drink. Then Mallory looked at him and shifted his gaze between the board and the small young man sitting in the empty classroom.

"Well, tell me I'm wrong," Mallory challenged, his voice forceful.

It started deep in Tishero — someplace around his guts — and moved slowly into his throat. Suddenly, like Mt. Fujiyama, it erupted into the space that separated the two men. "...Tess...Tess...Ra."

"Tesla...that's right. He knew and nobody else did. I didn't know you could talk." Mallory looked quizzically at the other man.

He signed back that he couldn't or never had been able to, but the shock of what he had just learned had caused something to happen inside him.

The debate went on, through Saturday morning and night and Sunday. By Monday morning they had run out of room on the whiteboards that circled the classroom and had started writing on the tile floor. The morning custodian opened the door at seven A.M. to find the two men writing down notes on sheets of paper spread across twelve desks. The room was littered with empty pizza boxes, hamburger wrappers, Hershey bar wrappers, three dead bottles of scotch, and one of sake. The men had great dark circles under their eyes and sat with their backs to the lectern, both reading from one book.

They had shared their lives, their hopes, their knowledge, and their beliefs for seventy hours straight only stopping to find a telephone and somebody that would deliver to the college.

By Monday morning, Tishero had come to a decision. He was going down to district court and change his first name to *Tesla*, and he was going to prove that all those equations on the board, desk, and floor could work. He had also learned to say two words — "Tess...ra" and "Mall...ray."

He spent the next six months like Mallory's shadow, in the lab and in the lecture hall, walking on beaches looking at sea shells, and reading the esoteric sections of every library he could find in a seventy-five-mile radius of Palo Alto. He dropped out of college and was often found with Mallory in a strip joint in San Francisco's North Beach. They sat in the back of the place, hunched over papers filled with equations, writing and signing. Mallory hooted and howled at the topless dancers and then would write down more figures. The now *Tesla* would run his hand through his thin black hair and pull at his thin black tie. He would frequently buy a table dance from one of the girls and point her toward some total stranger just to get her to go away and leave him and Mallory to work through the next step of the problem. They would walk over to Tosca's and listen to the opera music that came from the jukebox and sip cappuccino from small cups. Mallory would be holding three conversations with people at the same time, and then turn to look at Tesla's work and point to something. Then he'd take a pen from his pocket and write one or two lines and watch Tesla go into a diatribe of signing to the point that others nearby could swear that he was signing about Mallory's mother — again.

This was five years previous to the time that the

Mercedes Benz 450 SEL pulled into Clover Bay and parked in front of the office of Clyde Lindsey. The quiet oriental man with gray streaks in his hair walked into the office and bowed to the man behind the desk. Lindsey got up, stuck out his hand, and then felt like he had committed a great offense. He bowed twice and then Tesla bowed, both men bobbing like autonomous toys.

"May I help you?" Lindsey asked.

"Mallory?" the man said with another bow.

Lindsey started to bow and caught himself. "Figures," with a slight tone of exasperation. "Do you speak English?" The oriental repeatedly turned his head left to right.

"Then how the hell did you know I asked you if you spoke English?" Tesla pulled a card from his pocket and handed it to Lindsey. In four languages it explained that Tesla was mute, but could understand the spoken and written word in four languages.

"Oh...sorry." Lindsey found himself confronted again with a total contradiction. He looked out at the silver Mercedes. It had a rack added to the top, which was covered with what looked like a VanDeGraff generator he had seen in his high school physics lab. There was also a large coil of some kind. The inside was filled with gray equipment boxes and the trunk lid was held in place by a bungee cord. Odds and ends of equipment projected from inside.

By this time, Lindsey had made a few maps of the route out to Mallory's place and had them xeroxed for just such events. He pulled one from his drawer and handed it to Tesla. Tesla started to bow again as did Lindsey. Finally, Tesla shuffled out and got into his car. Lindsey noticed the California personalized license plate that simply spelled out "TESLA." As the car pulled out into the street it nearly missed one of the local dogs. The animal darted across the pavement with an iris plant in his mouth.

Mildred, the Post Master, was standing on the curb watching. She turned to Clyde who had walked outside his office and said, "That certainly doesn't sound like a Chinese name —*Tesla* — does it?"

"He's not. He's Japanese." Lindsey stood watching the red brake lights come on and off as the car spasmodically accelerated and decelerated up Main Street.

"Oh, that explains it." She walked passed him back down to the Post Office-cum-General Store-cum Mercantile Mart for Clover Bay.

"Sure it does." Lindsey walked back into his office and picked up a large amount of paper and files from his desk and dropped them into the metal garbage can next to his desk.

"New way of filing things?" The voice was Deputy Bob's.

"Actually, yes." Lindsey turned and looked at the man for a long moment. "What do you want?"

"I heard some talk about the ferry when I was up in Anacortes. Thought you might like to know."

"So?"

"They say that it looks like it's a goner for sure. It would take a real miracle to keep it running." Bob liked the feeling that information gave to him.

"Great...that's good to know Bob." Lindsey decided to go over to Harv's and get a shave. He walked past the deputy and out the door.

"You going to leave those files in the trash can?"

"That's not a trash can, it's a garbage can. There is a difference. Not that you would understand, but look up the definition in the dictionary sometime." With that, he walked across the street.

"Jesus, sorry about the news about the ferry. Didn't think it would upset you that much." Bob walked back to his patrol car and made a note in his log. He was even more convinced that Lindsey knew a lot more than he was saying.

CHAPTER 12

Clyde had checked his watch three times in half an hour. He remembered what Lady Lydia had told him about being late, and there was no way that he was going to be late on Friday night for dinner. Somehow, in his mind he knew that this evening was important, and he did not want to miss his destiny by not being at the Twitchell house at the appointed hour.

He had considered this for some time during the early afternoon. He was not sure why it had been so important for him to be there, but something about her had grasped him deep within what he thought of as his soul. Those eyes had captured him without contest. He knew that he had never met anybody like her, and he also knew that he had to know more about her.

He considered himself a simple man, yet this was not simple and he knew it. These were strange people, all of them. However, that strangeness attracted him like a moth to the flame of a candle. He could feel that this meeting could spell the end of this career as he knew it, or it could represent a new beginning that equally would be an end and a beginning. But whatever it meant he did not care. He only knew within his mind that he had to be there to see what all of this was about, and why he was so off balance every time he was around Mallory, Lady Lydia, or any of them. They held a strange captivation for him which he could not explain.

He walked from the rear entrance of his office-cum-home and stared at the two cars sitting side by side, his Toyota and her Citroen. Which would be proper to take to a dinner?

He thought that if he took hers he might have to walk home or again ask for a ride. That seemed strange to him, but then again, he felt the necessity to return the Citroen to her as he did not want to be responsible for keeping it at his place. He felt he was in the middle of a dilemma without even leaving his own confines.

He decided to take the Citroen. He opened the door and sunk into the dune-colored leather. He placed the key in the ignition and without turning it, the gauges came alive and the engine was running. He had not known that these cars were so advanced. He rolled down Main Street in the evening glow of the town. The car felt good under his hands. He was used to nice cars, he had grown up around them. However, this one seemed different to him. It handled differently. He looked across the dash and tried to find the radio. None. That seemed strange. A car that was this expensive did not have a radio.

"No music...." But before the soliloquy was done, the car was filled with the sounds of temple bells and chimes ringing in unison and forming a melody that was both haunting and wonderful. He noticed that one light on the dash was pulsating to the rhythm of the music. "Lower" — the sound reduced in intensity. "Higher" — the timbre of the notes increased. "Off" — and the car was filled with silence again. It was too much for him. He had heard about voice recognition for small computers, but this was really something completely new to him. He decided he would take a few moments to inspect the vehicle a little closer. Before he could touch the brake pedal, the car began slowing, and it pulled to the edge of Useless Bay Road. He looked for the dome light and found that it was on. He stared at it for a moment in his perplexity and then murmured, "Brighter...." The illumination factor of the dome light went up by 10 to 12 candle power. He ran his hand across the smooth dash trying to find a glove box — if there was one. He sat back and thought for a moment. "Open...." Suddenly the driver's side door swung out to the blaring horn of a truck that swerved to avoid hitting some damn fool's door that was jutting into the traffic lane. Lindsey sat there shaking for a moment after he had closed the door.

This was some kind of machine, all right. He recomposed himself and thought through the problem as carefully as he could. "Glove Box Open...." It was almost a whisper. Part of the dash slid sideways, revealing a large compartment with its own light recessed into the top. Inside was a black leather case.

He sat there and looked at it. This would be going a little too far. He felt like someone who had walked into somebody else's house and was going through their dresser drawers. This was not right. His morals and ethics were at odds with his driving curiosity to know what lay within that single black leather case in the glove compartment. This was intrusive, to say the least. His mind whirled. "What are you doing — more, what are you thinking about...?" He continued to mumble to himself. He sat there transfixed on the leather case. Would it reveal the answer to who she was and where she had come from? As he started to reach for the case, the passenger door opened. He looked up to see what invisible hand had pulled the latch. Then suddenly, a black blur bounced into the seat next to him. The cat sat and looked at him with his yellow eyes, and then stood and looked at the glove box. He looked back at Lindsey. The door swung closed and the cat gave out a small meow. The glove box door slid back into place and the cat sat down in the seat. Meowing again, the music came back on only softer this time. Lindsey sat there transfixed and staring at the road ahead of him.

"...Er...well...I just wanted to know something about...er." He looked down at the cat. "I am talking to a cat....I AM TALKING TO A CAT!" He hit the accelerator and pulled back out onto Useless Bay Road. "Get a grip, for Christ's sake. Now you're talking to cats and explaining to them what you're doing...this is not good, not good at all."

He sped down the road and finally turned into the gated drive. He studied the key pad. OPEN. What did that correspond to on a telephone key pad? He punched in four digits. Nothing. He tried another four. Nothing again. He sat back and tried to remember how the key pad on his telephone looked. "Let's see, one is ABC, two is DEF...."

The voice came from the speaker on the small gray box next to the key pad. "Why the hell don't you just use a petard and blow the son-of-a-bitch up, Lindsey?" Mallory's voice reverberated along the empty lane. "It's 6-7-3-6, you dolt."

"...Ah...thanks...6...uh...7-3-6. Okay...." The gate started to move back.

"Haddoxes could have told you that, but apparently you weren't listening." The voice drifted off as Lindsey drove up the driveway and parked in front of the house next to the Mercedes and Harley-Davidson. Well, this evening was starting out really well, Lindsey thought to himself as he stepped from the car and followed the cat up the stairs.

Lady Lydia stood by the open front door. She gestured for Lindsey to come into the house. Haddoxes walked by and looked up at her and meowed two or three times, rubbing up against her leg. She was dressed in a black dinner gown, which strapped over one shoulder and dropped below her other armpit. Black patent leather high heels and a gold hair clasp were the accents to her formal. "Please come in." She had that half smile on her face — like she knew the punch line to a joke nobody else knew.

"You look stunning...er...." Lindsey held out a small bouquet of flowers, which he had picked up over at the Mercantile, and fumbled with a wrapped bottle of wine.

"Oh, a little something simple for an evening at home. It's just a getup I wear when we have close friends in for dinner, nothing that would be appropriate for court." She took the flowers and placed them in a water-filled vase on the sideboard in the hallway then relieved him of the bottle of wine.

"Court?" Lindsey heard the word come out of his mouth, but did not realize that he had said it or what he was trying to find out.

"You know, all the snobs standing around and trying to one-up each other and make points with the Padashaw and all. Completely boring if you ask me, but on occasion necessary." She turned and walked into the living room. It had been completely rearranged and all the furnishings were back in place. It looked very much like he had remembered it when Margaret Twitchell had lived here.

"The equipment...you...er...Mallory has moved it someplace?" Lindsey felt himself losing his grasp on the ability to speak again. He remembered suddenly that he had been the debating champ in college and law school and now every time he was in her presence he could barely get a coherent statement out.

"They moved it to one of the shops out back. It

makes it a little better since Mr. T. arrived with his collection of toys."

"Mr. T.?" Lindsey wondered if someone else had shown up in town.

"Tesla, I believe you had the pleasure of meeting him the other day in your office. Small oriental man." She motioned to one of the chairs for him to sit in and he sat down. She perched on the edge of the overstuffed chair with her knees together, leaning forward. She was looking at him again with those star-filled eyes.

"Oh, yes. Nice gentleman. Doesn't say a lot." He did it again. The inside of his mind was screaming, 'Can't you say anything without sounding like a dummy, you jerk?' But he tried to regain some degree of composure. "But of course that is difficult for him."

"Sometimes words are hard for people, Mr. Lindsey. I have noticed that about your species." Before he could reply, Mallory came into the room, the smoke from his pipe whirling around him, and he was holding a set of computer printouts and mumbling into his beard. "Glad you figured out the gate, counselor."

"I couldn't remember the key pad on my phone." Lindsey felt that the sentence had come out in an appropriate manner.

"What the hell does that have to do with operating a touch pad on an electric gate? You know, Lindsey, you certainly show some signs of a man that has a bad case of Parthagenetic Personality Disorder. Your words don't go together very well and it would seem like there may be some Temporal Discontinuity occurring in your processor. But, what the hell....Lady Lydia thinks this will be a nice evening and so I am game for it. Let's eat." Without waiting for any response, he turned and walked toward the dining room that was across the foyer.

The table was set for five. A complete set of silver graced the table and white linen napkins adorned each plate. There was fine crystal next to each serving. A large bouquet of flowers filled the center of the table. Somehow it all seemed out of place to Lindsey when he looked at the man walking to the head of the table with an armful of computer printouts.

"What do you mean, Partagenetic Discontinuity?" Lindsey stood in the doorway.

Mallory turned and looked back at him. "Exactly. See how you place the wrong words in the wrong place almost every time. Dr. Pamela, down in Arizona — I think it's Tucson —has worked with people for years that do a similar thing. She found out that there is a disorder which she calls Parthagenetic Personality Disorder with Temporal Discontinuity. It is almost like a multiphasic disorder, but it is, in reality, temporally based in the cortex. Causes people to have anxiety attacks and panic, and also, when they are under pressure, they tend to use the wrong words in the wrong place. Brilliant girl. I tried to get the committee working on the DSM IV to acknowledge the condition and list it as a disorder. She is on the cutting edge. It's too new. The old hard-liners don't want to accept something this radical, and fifth columnist into the establishment. So they relegate her theories to less enlightened areas of the world. Like Arizona."

"Is it treatable?" Lady Lydia handed Lindsey a glass of champagne with a Thompson seedless grape in the bottom of the glass.

"Is what treatable?" Mallory had seated himself and lit his pipe. "Oh PPD. Of course. She uses a simple patch over the left eye. It affects the optical stimulation of the cortex, thereby preventing the subject from having the temporal discontinuity. They start to talk and think like normal people again, over night. It's amazing. Cognitive behavioralist. Jesus, I never thought that I would be calling some damn rat psycher amazing. But what the hell. She proved it so to me one night in a hot tub over a bottle of some grape-flavored German schnapps. Try it Lindsey. Put your hand over your left eye and say something intelligent."

Feeling like an absolute fool, Clyde put his hand over his left eye and stood there for a moment. "What am I suppose to say? I can't think of a thing that seems relevant."

"See....it works." Mallory looked down at his papers and repeatedly circled something with a red pen.

"What do you mean it works?" Lindsey was feeling as though he was the butt of some bad joke.

"Did you happen to notice that you never once in the last two sentences used the words 'aha' or 'er,' and that the sentences were complete and made sense? You really should consider wearing the patch for a month or so. It would do you wonders and probably increase your business because people would think that you knew what the hell you were talking about for a change. Are you planning to stand there all night and hold the champagne, or are you going to join us at the table and drink it?"

"Aha...well...excuse me. I thought...er...." Lindsey suddenly was aware of the fact the Lydia had also taken her place at the table and was sipping her drink. "Sure...thank you... I think."

From the back of the house came the sounds of pots and pans being dropped and the muffled sounds of someone swearing. Lindsey looked around at the door that led to the kitchen just as Ace walked through holding a large tureen of what smelled like soup.

"Ring the triangle, grub is served." Ace placed the dish on the table and disappeared back into the recesses of the kitchen.

"He is such an excellent chef. He could make a living at it if he would only apply himself." Lady Lydia mused to Mallory and then turned to look at Lindsey who had taken the seat across from her at the table.

"He could do a lot of things if he only applied himself, like fly. But no, he has to take the high road every time. Smells good. What the hell is it?" Mallory had the lid off and was stirring the brew clockwise.

"Curried mutton with wild rice." Ace was walking in with a large platter containing what looked to Lindsey like a leg of lamb covered with mint sauce. "A little leg of lamb, or as the old sheepherder's joke goes, 'a little piece of yew.'" He stepped back into the kitchen and reentered with a large dish of steaming vegetables. "And one more item for our close friend." Again he was gone. He came back with a serving plate covered with four different types of sushi and sat the plate next to Lindsey. He reached into his vest pocket and pulled out a pair of black with inlaid ivory chopsticks and placed them on the white dish.

"Now we can eat." He moved around and pulled out the chair next to Lady Lydia and sat down.

"Marvelous. It's about time, I'm starved." Mallory was already dipping into the curried mutton.

"Haven't you forgotten something?" Lady Lydia was looking at Mallory while he held a ladle full of curried mutton in the space between the tureen and his plate. A yellowish drip was forming at the bottom of the spoon and hung there waiting to desecrate the white linen table cloth.

"Oh yeah." He placed the spoon back in the dish before tragedy ensued.

Lindsey hung his head for what he knew must be the coming of a prayer or some kind of thanks. This only made sense to him. They seemed abrupt in so many ways, but looking at Lady Lydia, he knew that she must have some kind of religious belief that Mallory would honor. Lindsey thought of his own belief system, which was slim to none. He had convinced himself many years before that there was no God and no reason to thank anyone for something that he put on the table by the sweat of his own brow. But he felt that convention would be served if for no other reason than respecting this woman's belief system. So, in deference, he closed his eyes and thought to himself of how really beautiful she was and what it was about her that was so attractive. His reverie was unexpectedly interrupted.

"What the hell is wrong? Are you having some kind of aphasic attack, or are you just dedifferentiating into some kind of mindless boob that is going to pray over some poor dead piece of meat that is already starting to decompose and that we are planning to finish the job a little faster with our stomachs?" Mallory was looking at Lindsey as he raised his head and looked at the faces of the three people looking at him.

"I thought that you were going to pray or something...." He heard his words hang in the room.

"Jesus, Mary, and Joseph, what a putz. TESLA!" Mallory's voice echoed through the house like a loud speaker. The small oriental came into the room holding the twenty pound black cat and bowing.

He placed the cat on the table next to Lindsey and sat down. He was signing very quickly.

"Who cares, Tesla," Mallory retorted. "If the little son-of-a-bitch died, we would all be better off." The other man continued to sign.

Lady Lydia rebuked Mallory with a flash of her eyes. "You need him and he knows it, so I would be a little more accepting of him at this table."

"I don't need that little bastard one iota. Granted, he has helped with some of the scans on Zetta Four, but the price he extracts is far beyond the value?" Mallory said in a conciliatory way to Lady Lydia.

"Little value? You owe your left nut to him. Hell, without him we would have never been able to figure out what happened when the guy in Omaha went pan-dimensional and nobody saw him again for five years. Everybody and their brother thought it was an insurance scam. But no, he showed us how that little trick got played and why. You sold a hell of a lot of copies of your book because of that, and you don't think he is of value?" Ace had lit a Camel and was sitting with his elbows on the table, wagging his cigarette at Mallory.

"True, but he is such a mean little shit. I would just as soon shoot him in the head as to sit at the same dinner table with him." Mallory ladled a spoonful of curried mutton into Lady Lydia's dish then did the same for himself. He passed the tureen to Lindsey.

This was it. Lindsey had listened to enough. Holding the tureen and wondering how she could put up with this kind of abuse, he exploded. "The man may be a mute and a foreigner, but my God, he has feelings. You can't just sit here and say you'd rather shoot him in the head than eat with him, then just start to pass the food. Why did you invite him here if you were just going to denigrate him? I have never seen such a callous...."

"I didn't invite the bastard," Mallory was wiping some drippings from his beard. "I would never invite that scumbag to any place that I am working if it were not absolutely necessary."

"This is totally barbaric... you speak of ..." Lindsey couldn't remember Tesla's last name at all. "Mr....er... Mr. T. that way."

"Who the hell was talking about Tesla?" Mallory looked totally confused and moved his gaze from Lady Lydia to Ace across to Tesla and then finally back to Lindsey. "What are you talking about?"

"You just said that...." Lindsey started up again but was stopped by a raised hand from Lady Lydia.

"I think that there is a small misunderstanding here, Clyde." She pointed a long narrow finger at the cat, now being feed a piece of sushi by Tesla. "Mallory was not talking about Mr. T., he was referring to my traveling companion, Haddoxes. As I told you it's an old wound."

"You have some trouble with Temporal Discontinuity, fellow." Ace was looking hard at him. His blue eyes were like pieces of cold steel boring in Lindsey's face. "You may need to wear a patch over your left eye if 'n it gets worst, you know."

"What?" Lindsey turned and looked at a small oriental chewing a piece of red salmon wrapped around some white rice, and feeding the cat a bit and piece here and there from the ends of his chopsticks. "I thought you were talking about...."

"I have met smarter door knockers, counselor. Did you think I was speaking of my friend that way?" Mallory was now carving a piece of mutton from the leg and serving it with vegetables onto Lady Lydia's plate.

"Are you gonna hold the curried lamb all night, or take some and pass it over, buddy?" Ace was holding his hands out across the table. Lindsey hurriedly took two spoonfuls and passed the tureen.

"Sorry." Lindsey felt himself blushing at his last misdirected outburst of indignation. "But what's wrong with the cat beside the fact that it eats at the table?"

"What's wrong with the cat?" Mallory looked up as if seeking divine intervention.

"Protect us, oh Lord, from those that have eyes and cannot see. Try a patch over both eyes, that may help."

Lady Lydia was smiling at Clyde. "Ignore him. It is just green envy and jealousy that stirs a longing in him for that which he may never possess and that which Haddoxes has had."

This left Lindsey completely in the dark, but he felt it would be better not to show his ignorance this time by keeping all comments to himself. Surprisingly, the mutton was excellent. The dinner continued through three more courses, four bottles of wine, and two pots of coffee laced with cognac. By the time it was over, Lindsey was feeling light headed and was totally enjoying the badgering that ran around the table. Only once during the serving of the yellow chiffon cake with hard sauce did it get out of hand. It was when Mallory burst out with "Plex Dirot Gagma," to which Haddoxes spit and hissed, then went back to his corner of cake that smiling Tesla fed him with his chopsticks.

Feeling slightly tipsy, Lindsey decided to ask a question which had plagued him all night. "Is it normally the custom of this household to allow pets to eat at the table?" The silence was deafening. Not a face moved. Lindsey noticed that ten eyes were staring directly at him.

Mallory, in a very soft voice, leaned over and spoke to Lindsey. "You remember we had that little discussion the other day about what some people could call some people, and what they shouldn't call some people?"

Lindsey went in search of the neuron in his brain that held that holographic replication of that conversation. With the speed slightly less than the speed of light, the human brain can transmit an electro-chemical message between a neuron and the cortex and then equally as fast process it into verbal form, represented by speech in Lindsey's case, slightly slurred. "Oh yeah, you told me not to ever call...."

Mallory had put up his hand to stop Lindsey from speaking. "That's right...now, the same kind of rule applies to mentioning certain generic words that people like to apply to other life forms." Mallory was pointing to Haddoxes, who in turn was looking right into Lindsey's eyes. "There are certain life forms that find that being referred to as something which implies less than intelligent self-determination could be taken as an insult."

"The cat. You're talking about the cat!"

"Clyde, let's you and I go for a walk around the deck and look at the lights across the Bay." Lady Lydia was walking around to his side of the table.

"Oh...er...okay, that is fine by me." He started to get up, feeling his legs a little wobbly. "Great meal, Chef," he raised a thumb to Ace.

"Anytime, counselor."

Lady Lydia led him arm-in-arm out through the front door, their footsteps falling in unison on the deck to where the old porch swing hung.

"Counselor's a little bit into his cups, Doc," Ace was picking up dishes assisted by Tesla.

"Do you think what I think is going to happen right about now?" Mallory was looking into the distant past or distant future, but he was not in the now at all.

"Yep." Ace looked over at Tesla, who was giggling silently.

"Oh, Christ, is he ready for this?" Mallory pulled his pipe out and started to pack it.

"Nope." By this time, Tesla was almost doubled over in laughter, but not a sound came from him. "But Doc, we got something more important to talk about."

"What on earth could be more important than...,"

"Oh for pity's sake, it's only a figure of speech, you piece of Yxalic bait." With this the cat turned itself around in the chair and laid back down, not wishing to face the direction of Mallory.

"Something I found out about the other night from a really nice lady." Ace pulled one of the chairs out and parked himself next to Mallory. "We might as well get to work in the lab, 'cause nobody is going to get any sleep tonight in this house."

WAYNE E. HALEY

CHAPTER 13

The night air had cleared some of the alcohol-induced mist from between Clyde's ears. He and Lydia were sitting on the old porch swing that looked out across Useless Bay. The few lights on the other side shined like stars, reflecting and bouncing on the water. Lady Lydia moved the chair with an easy and gradual touch of her foot on the deck. Clyde sat with both feet off the deck, somewhat resembling a small child.

It has been often said that many a comment made while drunk was conceived while sober. Nothing could have been truer on this gentle fall evening in the great Northwest, for deep within the catacombs of Clyde Lindsey's mind a series of thoughts were starting to reform. The very nature of the atomic structure of his mind was taking on a new dimension. It was like the first time he had smoked grass in college. He turned to Lady Lydia and studied her profile in the half-light coming from the house.

"Where are you from?" His slur had lessened but was still slightly there.

"A long way away, Clyde." She was drinking in the night air and enjoying the shimmering lights on the Bay.

"Me, too. L.A. seems like a different planet to me now. God, am I glad I'm out of there." He fought down all the memories of why he left Los Angeles and the blue-eyed blond that had cost him half a beach house and half the savings account.

"I know the feeling, Clyde." She had that little half-smile on her face again.

"Do you like it here, I mean here in Clover Bay?" He tried to stay ahead of his thoughts for a change.

"It's all right. But all places are someplace to either go to or to come from. There are few places that seem like home." She reached out and took his hand and held it. Her skin was cold to his touch.

"You're cold; should we go in?" He started to move.

"No." She moved a little closer to him and put his arm around her shoulder. "It's different. I am, in fact, very warm right now." She turned and looked into his eyes. Her's were dancing with the lights of a thousand campfires on the old caravan trails from Marrakesh to Shimballa.

"I hope you plan to stay here for awhile because I would like to get to know you better. I just seem to make a damn fool out of myself all the time, so I wondered if...." His words trailed off as the caravan moved. He was left, not knowing the trade route.

"You're fine; it's just different being around them," she nodded with her head toward the house. "I have known them for years and we have an arrangement, but for an off-worlder it's difficult to understand."

"An off-worlder?" He struggled with his compass, wondering which way was north.

"A term, a phrase we play with for those who have not learned about things that Mallory and Ace and Tesla and myself talk about. It seems prejudiced, but that is not my intention with you, Clyde. It's just that you seem so innocent and naive, and Mallory has spent his life trying to educate people like you to a different way of thinking. He is concerned with what is called Critical Thinking. It requires one to take the opposite view of what they would normally feel comfortable with and defend it. It makes one think in different realities, and that is his strong point." She moved closer to him. He could smell the perfume that had hints of jasmine and orange.

"I find that I really like you, Lydia." The words hung for a moment then disappeared like mist in the wind. All the cautions Mallory had given him about informalities were vague images hiding in the corners of his mind and not to be found. She pulled away, turned and looked deep into his eyes. He started to speak, realizing his error. She placed a finger on his lips and shook her head slowly.

"In the place that I come from there is an herb. Tracistain. It is for lovers. It allows them to...," she thought through her words very carefully "...to maintain their excitement for a period of twelve to fourteen hours. It should never be taken while alone, for it would lead to irreparable damage to both body and mind. But when those that find each other accommodating take it together, there is a magical blending of their essences into a creative force that is shuddering to behold. Certain Tibetans have found a similar herb in the high mountain passes. They secret it away in lamaseries and temples. At one time, it sold for more than gold in the bazaar of Samarkan. To possess it was the gift of life to those whose hearts and bodies had grown old. Men have killed for it and stolen for it. They've sold their children, families, and worldly belongings, and no one that has ever taken it is ever the same again."

Her words were hypnotic to him. The rhythm and timbre of her voice touched a part of him long dormant. She took his hand and placed two small capsules in his palm. "If you are to have courage and seek that which you desire in this life, you must first undergo some form of initiation. All great, and most lesser religions, cults, and theologies teach that." She looked at him questioningly. "Are you prepared to leave this world behind and join those of us that have seen the Stygian Triangle?"

His mind raced. Was she one of Mallory's patients? Was this some rare kind of madness that he had never seen? Or was this a game that these folks played to entertain bored minds? What was in the pills? LSD, coke, PCP, or some designer drug? He looked into those eyes and wondered. His thoughts mixed with a lifetime of not knowing anything but believing in much. He looked into those blue-within-blue eyes filled with the stars of the universe and questioned.

• • • • •

"There are two great mountains separated by a deep gorge. Across this gorge is an ancient rope-and-timber bridge. One mountain is ignorance, the other mountain is knowledge, and the bridge is your life. If you walk across the bridge, the timbers will fall out one by one with each step that you take, and when you reach the other side, there will be no way of resuming to ignorance. You now stand at the threshold of that bridge, Clyde. What is it you want to do?"

He looked at her again and felt a burning pain inside. It was that part of him that he had pushed into a little box years ago and put up on a shelf in his mind, never to be opened again. In that box was vulnerability, care, and something called love. But he had told himself that once in any lifetime was enough to play with such a caustic acid. It had burned him, and because of that he had relegated it to the box and thence to the shelf in the closet in his mind.

"I want you...." The words poured out without

his control.

She lifted one capsule from his palm, held it up to her mouth and swallowed it. She closed her eyes for a moment and then opened them again. He still held the other pill in his hand. She took it between her thumb and index finger and put it to his mouth. He opened his mouth and she laid it on his tongue. She gently put her finger to his lips and then, while still touching him, she leaned forward and kissed him. The water of life coursed through his veins.

Someplace in the limbic system of Clyde Lindsey's mind an explosion took place. His mind was filled with the illumination of a hundred thousand suns all at once, and his consciousness was spread across the universe. It expanded and contracted until his very fiber and being was pulsating to the hidden and secret rhythm of the dance of a hydrogen atom. He was part and total all at the same time. His mind opened and the occult knowledge of all shamans, seers, and vision-questors poured into it; and the songs of a thousand chants resonated within his very being. Above Clover Bay a large fireball of a meteorite was seen arching through thirty degrees of sky.

CHAPTER 14

The light filtered into the room. The sun on the east side of the house was creeping around the corners of the big old place and only the random, reflective light was pouring into the bedroom on the west side of the house. Clyde Lindsey lay naked in the big old brass bed that had once been Margaret Twitchell's. The down comforter was warm and snug over him. He was laying there listening to the birds sing in the early morning air. He was watching the movement of the leaves in the treetop next to the house. The old alder must have been thirty years old. That is old for an alder tree he thought. He concentrated on that thought. How did he know that this was old for a tree of this kind? Hmm...must have been something that he heard someplace along the line. He sat straight up in bed. Where in the hell am I? What am I doing in Margaret Twitchell's old brass bed? Where are my clothes? A hundred more dislocated questions ran through his totally confused mind. I was having dinner last night and we were talking about the cat....The sun moved two degrees in the sky before the next thought came through his head. God, I must have been really drunk. I hope I didn't make a complete ass out of myself. He started to get up and found that his legs would not support him. Every fiber of muscle ached. Boy, it has been awhile since you got this blitzed. The little voice inside continued the silent dialogue with his external self. How in the hell am I going to go downstairs and look these people in the face? What if I did something really stupid? What if I made a pass at Lydia? ...Lydia? Mallory told me never to call her Lydia.... I was not initiated into that fratern... his mind seized up again. What if...?

Lindsey walked into the kitchen where Ace was working on the leg of lamb. He was using a Buck knife to trim the meat away from the bone. He hummed some little ditty while he worked. "You don't use regular kitchen knives for a task like this?" Lindsey halfway pointed to the leg of lamb and plate piled high with slices next to it.

"Nah, learned how to do this from a Basque up around Gardnerville, Nevada. He ran a place that served good food and lots of it, but he never gave up his traditions from back home. You'd always use a hunting knife to clean a bone really well." Ace handed Lindsey a piece of cold mutton and he started to nibble at it. "You're pretty square, aren't you, counselor?" Ace was wiping the Buck knife on a towel and pulling a Camel from his pocket. "No offense meant."

"None taken. Yeah, well...er...until the last couple of months, I would say that I was about as square as a Mormon bishop at a Shriners' Convention." Lindsey walked over and took a cold can of cola out of the refrigerator and popped the lid.

"Oh, it's okay; it's just that some of us have lived a little different life, and I think sometimes that makes us a bit rude to be around." Ace flipped the Buck knife into the cutting board and poured a cup of coffee into a blue enameled mug. He pulled a chair out and sat down. Propping his feet up on the corner of the kitchen table, he stared at Lindsey for a moment. His clear blue eyes appraised him. "What is it, old son, that you want to ask?" The silence fell around the room until the only sound was the intermittent dripping of the water in the sink.

"Am I that transparent?" Lindsey leaned against the counter and picked up another piece of cold lamb and started to munch on it.

"Let's just say that I got a knack for being able to read folks." Ace lifted the cup to his mouth and paused. "It's not that you're more or less transparent; it's just people get this funny way about them when something is bugging them and they don't know how to ask."

"You don't seem to suffer from that problem and neither does Mallory. Good grief, you two are about as direct as any two people I have ever met."

"Oh, hell, we're just rude bastards that don't know better. We've spent too much time in the back of the pucker brush where, if you weren't direct, somebody would put you in a pot and you'd be dinner for a week." Ace laughed to himself at the image of being in a cannibal pot with his hat still on. "So, come on, tell Uncle Ace what it is that's got you all in a lather."

"Well...er...ah...it's...ah...Lydia...Lady Lydia. I wanted to know if she and...well, let's see here...ah...." Lindsey was studying the top of the pop can to the point that he could have described the molecular structure of it and the way the ions went together.

"Nope. Her Highness and Mallory have never been an item in the way you are thinking. They are good friends and have been, and do take care of each other in many ways." Ace was sitting there with that "go-ahead-and-trust-me" smile.

"Well, that is not what I meant, really...." Lindsey turned and looked out the window.

"Sure it is. And moreover, you were wondering if there was a professional relationship between them. You know, like doctor and patient. Right?" Ace's smile increased in proportion to Lindsey's discomfort.

"Well...er...yeah, I guess so." Lindsey was still looking out across the backyard at the maple tree. "I also wanted to know how they met.... She is so remarkable and Mallory is...er...."

"Sit down, old son, 'cause I am going to tell you a story, the likes of which you'd have a hard time finding on the fiction shelf, let alone anyplace else." Ace got up and poured another cup of coffee and sat back down across from Lindsey. "Don't interrupt and don't ask any questions for awhile, and I'll put a lot of this in fine perspective for you."

Lindsey sat down and watched the change in Ace's face. It went into kind of a mask, the way storytellers sometimes do when they are remembering something from a long time ago.

Ace's voice started out with a soft and slow kind of sound, like a mother talking to her baby. "It was back around 1947, down in the Southwest. It seemed like lots of people were trying to improve things after the war. The boys had come home and lots of folks were talking about scientific stuff — rockets, A-bombs, and jets. Out at Muroc Air Base, they were trying to get that X-1 to fly past the sound barrier, but it had a way of burying pilots — that old demon that lived out in the thin air at Mach One.

"Over in New Mexico, near Roswell, was where the old 509th Bomb Group was stationed. That was the only atomic group in the country. It's where Tibbets and his crew came from." Ace watched Lindsey move in his chair and put a hand up to calm him. "It all fits together, you'll see." He pulled another long drink from his coffee. "There are no simple answers. You will learn that. Well, let's see...oh, yeah. That country down there is known for its hellish thunder and lighting storms that come up from the south in late summer. The morning will be clear and the afternoon will build up; by four or so, the sky will be gray and electricity will be pulsing and slamming all around. A ship, a scout ship from Stygia, was snooping around the 509th, trying to find out what the latest advances were. It got caught in a hell of a storm. One thing you find out pretty early when you start to investigate UFOs is that they run on electricity. All the circuits and drive systems are electrical. So when you are inside an atmosphere like ours, and you find that you got an electrical storm around you, it's a good idea to hightail it out of the way.

"Well, it was too late. A lightening bolt came up from the ground and short-circuited just about everything on the craft. It was going tits up in the worst way. The pilot had just enough time to send an alert and request for help. And then they plowed up about two miles of ranch land and busted all to hell in a wash about thirty-five miles north of Roswell on a ranch. Well, this rancher, Brazel, I think that's his name, come over and took a look at the crash site, saw the craft, some of the folks inside it, and he headed for town." Ace lit a cigarette and blew smoke up towards the ceiling. Like an old fortune-teller, he was looking into the smoke to see if the shapes and forms would collect to make a picture.

"You telling me that the story about the crash at Roswell of the UFO is true?" Lindsey was waiting for the punch line.

"Yep." Ace looked across and smiled. "Want to hear the rest?"

"Does it come to a current event sometime?" Lindsey found himself annoyed again at the smiling cowboy.

"It will but it takes time, like a great meal being prepared." Ace got up. "But if you got something better to do...."

"Not a thing." Lindsey now knew he wanted to know where all of this was going.

"Okay. Well, while Brazel was heading towards town and to a phone, a royal diplomatic ship heard the distress call. The rule in the quadrant is that all ships come to each other's aid when they are having trouble on a non-advanced planet. Wreckage and bodies upset the civilians when they read about them in the morning papers. They start thinking that they are not alone in the universe.

"So this diplomatic ship leaves its course and comes on in, hell-bent-for-leather, trying to save anybody that they can and clean up the mess, if that's possible. Well, lo and behold, the same killer storm that blew the scout ship outta the sky pegs the diplomatic ship in its drive core, and suddenly you got two alien crafts that are going to be permanent residents on this type-M planet.

"Bam! About three miles from the first crash the second ship hits and zaps the whole crew with the exception of the navigator and the only passenger on the ship besides the crew. The navigator is that little piece of black and white fur around here, and the passenger is Her Worship, The Royal Lady Lydia...," he trailed off for full effect.

"Wait one minute." Lindsey was leaning

forward in his chair. "That was over forty years ago that happened. She could have only been a child, or worse — a baby...."

"Nope, full grown like now." Ace smiled again.

"Ah...um...that would make her...ah...seventy, at least. Impossible!" Lindsey started to get up, but Ace pointed for him to sit back down.

"You wanted to know. Now just sit there and listen." He looked into his coffee cup and back at Lindsey. "She is closer to eighty-five right now, but just doesn't show it a lot. Anyway, she was pretty busted up in the crash. Haddoxes was beside himself. It was his job to get her where she was going and to protect her in the meantime. He was not doing a really good job at the time. About this same time, folks from the Army Air Corp started showing up at the other crash site and picking up bits and pieces of the craft. They carted the bodies off to the air base. Well, Haddoxes was going rat-ass crazy. The Royal Lady Lydia was knocked out and he had to make some fancy moves. He grabbed her and what effects he could carry, and started to beat feet up toward some hills. He figured that he could make a stand up there if worse came to worse."

Just about then, the door pushed opened and Haddoxes came into the kitchen. He jumped up on the counter, looked at the tray of lamb and sat down. He looked at Lindsey then Ace. "Knew we were talking about him, the little rascal."

"You're telling me that this twenty-pound cat

picked up Lydia and some survival stuff and headed cross country?" He looked at Haddoxes, who just meowed at him and then at Ace. "I don't know who is crazier, you or me — you, for telling the story, or me for sitting here and listening. But what the hell, go ahead."

"Well, he made a camp and then headed back to the first crash site. By this time, Major Jack Martelle was there — a really good man by all accounts; he was the one that broke the story that a UFO had crashed. It didn't take long for "The Cult of Silence" boys to show up and start scaring the hell out of everyone involved. They denied the story of the crash and claimed that it was a weather balloon. Then they spent some time talking to everyone that had seen anything, and convinced them that they would take anybody that talked about the crash out into the desert on a one-way ride.

"They had taken the bodies to the base and were going to perform an autopsy on each of them and film them. They did this at the base hospital and used some of the staff. Then they threatened to kill them if they talked to anyone about exactly what had happened. The rest of the guys from The Cult were down at the hanger loading up all the parts and pieces of the ship, and putting it on trucks heading for Wright Patterson Air Base in Dayton, Ohio, the home of the Cult.

"Ole Haddoxes there, he strolled into the base hospital just like he belonged and started to look around. Well, sure in hell they had taken those aliens apart piece by bloody piece, and most of them were in body bags or glass jars filled with alcohol. It was not a pretty sight. Haddoxes was moving along the edge of the corridor when he picked up the vibes of one of the civilian doctors that had been pressed into service by the military. He was an older man, a Dr. Atwood — a semiretired surgeon who lived in Roswell and who had been a military doctor during the war. He was standing in the hall while a security guy was reading him the riot act about if he talked to anyone, or if he wrote any of this down and telling him what was going to happen to him and his family. He had been pressed into all this because he held a reserve officer status in the military and he had little or no choice. But Haddoxes could tell by the feelings that he was putting off, that this job was not to his liking.

"Atwood was leaving the base. It was late in the evening and he wanted to go home, take a bath, and have a good stiff drink. He was going to try really hard to forget what he had seen and what he had done. He had already figured out that somebody had decided that they didn't want anybody outside the Cult to know about the ships, the aliens, or the crash. That much was clear. So Atwood got into his old Chevy and was getting ready to leave when he looked down and saw a small set of yellow eyes looking up at him. He wondered for a moment how the cat had gotten into his car and how long it had been there. He was just about to pick it up and put it outside when the frontal lobe of his brain started to resonate. A billion or so neurons fired at the same time and Dr. Atwood, for the first time in his life, experienced telepathy.

"The message was very simple. 'We need your help and we can not allow what just happened to happen to a royal person.' Well, needless to say, Atwood was beside himself. He thought that he had worked too long in the room with the strange smell, and the ether might have had an effect on him, coupled with the trauma of the day, the setting, the secretiveness of the Cult, all of it. But then it came again, 'We need your help.' He stared at the cat for a long minute and suddenly an image was born in his mind of what a shape-shifter looks like when it is not a cat. He repelled across the seat and hit the door with a bang. He could not move because of sheer fright.

"The voice came again inside his skull. 'We won't hurt you, we just need your help.' He was sweating badly by now, and the lingering image of the red eyes of the shape-shifter was boring into his mind. He could not reconcile this image to the cat that was sitting in the seat next to him. 'We do not wish to hurt people, but we can not let them touch a royal personage, not like this.' The flooding images of the autopsy of the aliens rushed back into Atwood's mind. He saw every incision and cut that he and the other surgeon made. He smelled the toxic blood and accumulation of fluids in the viscera of the alien scouts that died. He saw the small captain that had told him what would happen to him if he spoke to anyone about this. And yet, he looked into those yellow eyes and was compelled to respond. He straightened himself and started to drive out the front gate. The cat sat beside him and watched him as he drove. After passing through the main entrance, he found himself starting to talk to the cat like it was a human. 'Where do you want me to go?' The answers came quick and precise from Haddoxes — a navigator in space or on land.

"Atwood drove up to the Brazel place and turned in on the old dirt road. There were still sentries there that stopped him and told him he couldn't go any farther. He pulled out his military ID and told them that he was part of the medical team from the 509th, and that he had been instructed to go back out to check and see if there was anything else that he could do. The sentries were not completely sure what it was they were guarding, but this man was military, so they let him through. Plus the fact that he was an officer, and nobody of an enlisted rank ever thought it a wise idea to question an officer too much.

"Atwood drove as far as he could on the Brazel Ranch and then stopped the car, got out and started to follow the cat as it walked north towards the low rolling hills. It took about a quarter of an hour to get up to the small indention that Haddoxes had used for a shelter, and where he had laid The Royal Lady Lydia away from the sun and wind.

"Atwood immediately dropped to one knee and started to examine her for injuries. He turned slowly to see the seven feet of the shape-shifter looking at him. 'I meant no disrespect. I am a doctor, and in our culture on this world, people like me are responsible for the health and care of our people. This is the examination that we must do to determine the injuries and the extent of the trauma.' With that, he received Haddoxes's permission to continue touching her. Without that permission, Haddoxes would have ripped him limb from limb — just as he did to that old sheep." Ace stopped to get another cup of coffee.

Lindsey stared at the cat. He had rolled onto his side and looked at the counselor with those small yellow eyes. He meowed again. "Nice kitty." Lindsey reached over him and picked up another piece of mutton, looked at it and put it back.

Ace sat down and lit another Camel. "The doctor determined she had a bad head injury. But not knowing her anatomy, he wasn't sure how bad it was. He knew one thing. He'd be damned if he was going to let her lie there all night, or if any of those bastards at the base were going to get their hands on this woman. He picked her up and turned to head back toward the car, only to be faced by the shape-shifter again. This time, though, something had happened inside Atwood. He stood toe-to-toe with the most fearsome creature in this galaxy — the one feared and banned on half the civilized planets of this galaxy. 'Do what you wish, but she is going back to my house and office where I can treat her properly and make her well. So either do your damnedest to me, or get the hell out of the way. Pick up those things that she needs and serve her like you are supposed to, you hair bag.' With that, the doctor walked right around Haddoxes and down to the car without another word of complaint from the navigator.

"He was driving off Brazel's ranch when he ran directly into Major Martelle. The Major had come out to look around again and found out that the doctor was there snooping around. Martelle walked up to the passenger side and opened the door seeing her Ladyship lying on the front seat. He looked over at Atwood and at the small black cat in the backseat. Martelle started to reach for her wrist to take a pulse. In a low voice, Atwood said, 'Do not do that Major, not if you value your life and mine.' Martelle stopped and looked up at the doctor and then back into the yellow fixed eyes of the cat. 'Doctor you can't take her away from here, you know that.' Atwood didn't flinch a muscle. He just slowly turned to Martelle and their eyes met. 'Do you want to be responsible for her lying on a stainless steel table back at the base and watch while one of those butchers cuts her apart piece by piece?'

"'They'd try to save her. She could be of great help to explain what is going on here and where all of those creatures came from.' Martelle stood transfixed, looking down at her face. 'You know as well as I do, that you brought in two of those other creatures alive. They are now parts of a biological experiment on its way to Wright-Patterson — in pieces.' Martelle stepped back from the door and said, 'Are you telling me that those guys killed them?' Atwood looked forward through the window at the two curious guards that were watching the doctor and the Major as they talked to each other. 'On my mother's grave, I am telling you that ether was given to the point that the respiratory system stopped working. And that it was done with the knowledge and intent that those two aliens were not meant to wake up, ever.' Atwood turned again and looked at Major Martelle. 'Your call, Major.'

"Martelle stepped back from the car and closed the door. He walked around to the driver's side and leaned down. 'Drive safely going home, doctor, and maybe I will stop by and see how your 'niece' is doing in a few days.' Atwood put the car in gear. 'That would be fine Major, you are always welcome.'

"Well, he took her back to his place. He had a big older home in town with a small office/clinic attached to it that was pretty well equipped for '47. He put her in a small room that was just off the clinic and started to perform some tests on her. All of this was under the watchful and discerning eye of that fuzz bag up there on the counter. Atwood was a widower and didn't have any children, so his days were passed in seeing his normal routine of patients, and the nights spent nursing his charge back to health. She was in a coma for almost three months. But finally, one rainy night in February, she opened her eyes and looked at the silver-haired man who was asleep in the chair next to her with a book in his lap.

"She noticed Haddoxes sitting in the corner and commanded him to explain what had happened and where she was. He told her that he had moved as many of her belongings as he could into the basement, and salvaged as much of the equipment off the ship before he destroyed it, so that no one could lay their hands on it. He explained that they were marooned on this M-type planet, a hundred light-years from her home. She looked at the room and then lifted the covers and examined her body. Haddoxes turned to face the wall when she asked all the embarrassing questions as to whom or rather what had touched her. She looked at the man asleep in the chair and suddenly realized that she owed her life to him, and that she was going to be here for a good long time.

"Time went by. She learned the language, customs, and cultures of our land. Atwood kept her at the house and just told people that she was a niece on his late wife's side, and that she was a little odd due to the fact that she had been raised on the East Coast. In New Mexico, saying that was like telling somebody that the person was from a distant planet. They understood immediately why the dark-haired lady was strange. Weren't all folks from New Jersey or New York weird? She kept up the pretense for many years, reading, learning, traveling and taking in all that she could to see what made up this small blue planet.

"Over the years, she grew to love Atwood and helped him in the clinic as he grew older. Atwood had strong feelings for this woman that became a complete part of his life. He spent his days in the clinic around her and nights by the fire, reading and talking to her, sharing everything that he could with her. I truly believe he forgot that she was not of our world. She was part of him. The community grew to love her, too. They constantly invited her to functions, to which she politely declined, yet every one had something nice to say about her.

"Then sometime around '70-'71, Atwood was listening to the radio. A talk program came on with a bright young graduate student discussing contact with other life forms and the need to protect them and make sure the Cult of Silence didn't get to them first. Atwood took great pains to find out everything he could about the speaker and even went so far as to hire a private detective in San Francisco to put together a dossier on the man. After reading the dossier and finding all that was in it was positive according to the way Atwood looked at the world, he sent a brief note and a map to an address in Berkeley.

"Three days later, a dark green Dodge station wagon pulled up outside and a pipe attached to a human face walked up the sidewalk and knocked on the door of the clinic. Atwood stuck his hand out and pulled the man inside. For the next three days the man read twenty-three years of diaries and journals that the doctor had kept. Sleeping in the guest room for about three hours a night and locking himself in the doctor's study the rest of the time, he didn't speak to Lady Lydia or the doctor until he was finished. He walked out at seven o'clock in the evening of the third night and looked at her Ladyship and simply stated, 'I'm Dr. C. Thomas Mallory and I am at your service.'" Ace got up and washed his cup and dried it. He started to put the mutton away in the refrigerator.

"That's it, the whole story, right there?" Lindsey was moving around the kitchen like a dervish.

"Of course not, but that is how they met. He has been with her ever since." Ace turned and looked into the middle space where memories are kept. "Atwood was dying; he knew that there should be someone, a mentor, a friend, someone. He liked what he saw in Mallory and trusted him. So he told him the whole story with her permission.

"Doc did what he has always done. He looked for the reality, found it, and dedicated himself to the mission — that of being a friend to a visitor. He has been there for her, never pushing in, but always there for assistance, comfort, and to help her when the true loneliness of being on a strange planet far away from home pushes in. They are more like brother and sister than anything else. He acts like he is indifferent, but that is one man you would not want to see if someone showed disrespect for her Ladyship."

Lindsey sat transfixed in the kitchen now, looking at the cat just sitting there. "Martelle knew. He knew she was here all the time and he never said anything."

"That's right. Until he died, and nobody in the family ever said anything either, 'cause I think they knew, too." With that, Ace walked out of the kitchen and Lindsey was left alone with old memories and a small cat looking at him.

• • • • •

Mallory was sitting at the dining room table with a notepad and pen, working with a small calculator when Lindsey walked into the room. He never looked up from his calculations. "Coffee is on the sideboard and have a Danish." Lindsey noticed the stack of cups and selection of Danish. They did not look like the ones Gracy's Bakery sold. Her's were more like hockey pucks. These were really light and fluffy. He took two of them and a cup of hot black coffee. He sat down next to Mallory, trying to see what he was working on. The sheet of paper was covered with numbers and letters all mixed together in various forms of equations. Mallory finally finished whatever he was doing and looked up and took a sip of coffee.

"Do me a favor." It was neither a question nor statement. "On the noon ferry, there will be a young blond woman coming off the boat. Would you go into Clover Bay and pick her up and bring her out here?"

"Sure." Lindsey finished his Danish and wiped his mouth. He started to leave the room, then turned back to Mallory. Before he could speak, Mallory was up and walking into the kitchen mumbling something from his pad. "Take the Dodge, it will be easier on you for curiosity sake."

"How will I know her?"

"You'll know." He was gone into the kitchen. Lindsey walked down the porch steps and out on the lawn. He had never noticed the flagpole before. It struck him that there had not been a flagpole at the house. This was something new. Flying from it was a fluorescent pink flag. Ace was standing thirty feet away looking at it, transfixed. Lindsey walked over to him and commented. "Strange type of flag."

"I love it. It is the Stygian Flag. I love those three colors." Ace was staring directly up at it.

"It's only one color."

"It's a pink flag with a pink field on it, and the pink Stygian Triangle in the corner, you dolt. It's three colors." Ace finally turned and looked at Lindsey.

"My mistake, sorry." Lindsey turned to walk away. It just seemed to him like one color, but who was he to argue with someone that even knew what the flag was. He drove the Dodge station wagon into town with Tina Turner screaming at the top of her lungs. He thought to himself, what a really nice day.

CHAPTER 15

Lindsey arrived back in Clover Bay about 10 A.M. He had time to stop by his office and check his answering machine. The woman that wanted to know if she could be sued because her dog dug up the neighbor's iris bed had left another message. This time it was about a rose bed of some kind. Two messages were from members of the County Planning Commission about a proposal that was due in next week that Lindsey was supposed to be working on. And one was from somebody wanting to know if he knew anything about a strange pink flag flying at the north end of the Bay. He rewound the tape and erased all of the messages.

He looked through the stack of files and found the proposal for the County Commission. He read through it, struggled to put it into an envelope, sealed it, addressed it, and walked on down to the Post Office. Mildred was there and she looked up from behind the counter when he walked in. "Post Office is only open Monday to Friday, 8 to 5."

"But you're here," Lindsey held up the package.

"Not my rules, United States Postal Commission rules." She was reading the newspaper.

"Right." Lindsey walked over to the scales and weighed the envelope. "If you were to sell me any stamps, it would require a buck-fifty worth of stamps, Mildred."

"Can't sell them; it's the rule." Mildred turned the page on the weekly paper and read the next column of gossip.

"Could you loan me a dollar-and-fifty cents worth of stamps so I can put this package in the mail chute? Now, that won't break the law, will it Mildred?" Lindsey stood there holding the parcel like it was a fragile Dresden doll.

"I could if I had some, but since they are all locked up behind the postal counter, I don't have any except for those in the machine over there that we sell to the tourists for their post cards." She continued her survey of who had died and, more importantly, why.

Clyde walked over to the machine. It dispensed blocks of one dollar's worth of stamps for one dollar and twenty-five cents. He fumbled in his pocket and pulled out three quarters. He then opened his wallet and extracted two one-dollar bills, which he laid on the counter. "Could I get some quarters, please?"

"Not a bank, either." Mildred had always been known for the attitude that she was now showing in perfect form.

"Yes, but I do wish to use your machine." Lindsey felt a degree of frustration arising within him. Was it a feeling he had just chosen to ignore in the past, or was there some new way of looking at his world that made him feel like this was a really bad Candid Camera sketch being played out in front of his eyes?

"Well, since you're planning to spend it here, I guess...." She pulled herself away from the article about the missing sheep and walked over to the postal booth. She took out eight quarters from the drawer and replaced them with the two bills.

"You said it was closed, rules and all that...," Lindsey held the quarters she had put in his hand.

"Yeah, it is, but those have the red paint on them so I can keep track of which ones go into the machine." Mildred returned to the tale of the raiding Indians that had stolen nearly half a flock of sheep.

Lindsey started to speak then thought better of it, and went to the machine and watched it gobble up his offering. It dispensed the two packages of stamps. He placed all of them on the envelope.

"That's too much, it's wasteful." Mildred eyed him as he tossed the package into the chute marked "local."

"You can't worry about that today, Mildred. It's not on Postal Service time." He turned without waiting for a reply, and walked out into the sunlight.

· · · · ·

The noon ferry had just arrived in Clover Bay. It was 11:09 A.M. Clyde figured that was about right. Call it the noon ferry and get it here about an hour early. That made perfect sense, much like everything here. He noticed Deputy Bob standing on the pier, waiting to see the various folks walk off the ferry. He was in his best undercover outfit doing covert surveillance. That meant he had on his blue jeans that were pleated down the front, and his plaid shirt. The bottom of his holster was sticking out from underneath the hem of his shirt. He was holding a copy of the weekly newspaper and watching over the top — his best Inspector Clouseau impersonation. He was always there on Saturdays to look for questionables coming off the boat. He knew that those folks coming up from Seattle to Clover Bay needed watching, 'cause some of them were "hippies" involved in illegal "things." Nobody could ever really get a definition of hippies or illegal things out of Bob, but he knew.

It had never struck Clyde before today, but he suddenly realized what a total waste of manpower, in fact, what a total waste of taxpayers' money it was to have this clown stand around and watch innocent people trying to get away to have fun. Clyde struggled and walked past him down to the dock. "Careful, Bob, I heard a rumor that Samuel Clemens is on the ferry today."

"REALLY? Oh, well...thanks Mr. Lindsey. I'll keep an eye out for him." Bob straightened up and started to use his trained observer abilities that much more.

Lindsey was chuckling to himself as he walked up next to the boat and watched as the passengers, mostly couples, descended the gangway. He had already put some zinc oxide on his nose to prevent sunburn. The only way anybody was going to get sunburned in fall in the Pacific Northwest was if they stood under an infrared bulb for an hour. But it added to the aura of the great out-of-doors.

He kept looking for someone that was blonde and blue eyed. The normal groups were there, folks with backpacks and rucksacks, all wanting to get a little bit of nature into their weekend. He was caught by the sight of one of them.

The last passenger had left the boat and a few tourists and locals were boarding for the ride up to Friday Harbor in the San Juan Islands. The great whistle blew and the ferry pulled away from the ramp leaving Clyde Lindsey standing there looking at it as it churned the water into a white cauldron. "Must not have been on it."

He turned to walk back up the dock and found that a woman dressed in black and white blocked his path. The five-foot-eight woman was about a hundred-and-fifty pounds under the black and white robes of the Roman Church. She was holding two bags, a small leather traveling case, and a large bag that looked like a fiberglass case.

· · · · ·

As she walked down the plank from the ferryboat, she looked around at the village. Her mind went back in time to how this journey had begun. (Her thoughts were in German, but since only three percent of general readers know the German language, the author took the liberty to put them into English...but it should be noted that the original thoughts were not of that language. However, that leads into the discussion of language and thought. If Carl Gustav Jung was correct, then thought is archetypical and not language restricted — another story.)

She remembered coming over from the old country to work as an assistant at a retirement home for older sisters. She had thoroughly enjoyed her work until the night that one of the retired sisters had awakened her to look at the bright light coming in the second floor window. She had watched the light change color and then take on shape. She soon observed that it was a craft of some kind. It was something out of her realm of understanding, yet it was real.

She had watched over the next few days as the group of "investigators" had showed up. These were professional people that did not receive any compensation for their work, but rather did it because they, as she did, wanted to know answers to questions that seemed to have no logical explanations. She had remembered the attractive petite blond teacher who had spent so much time talking to everyone involved, and walking over the grounds where they had seen the light. She had watched as the woman and her associates had taken soil samples from the large marking in the area where the craft was seen hovering. She recalled that the marking on the ground was the shape of a half-circle, and that the soil in that area had the consistency of flour; it was totally dehydrated. The grass was still somewhat yellowish and flattened. As she recalled the incident in her mind's eye, she could still see the investigators carefully placing these samples into small plastic containers and marking each one carefully.

She had asked one of the German-speaking sisters if these people were from the government. It only seemed right to her that anybody doing this type of investigation had to be a government agent. But the answer was "No." They were from a private organization that studied these strange occurrences. She found that her nights were now plagued with a thirst for knowledge.

Books by the German writer about chariots were her constant companions. She didn't know if he was right or just a good fiction writer. She needed to know more. The gray walls of the cloister were pushing in too much for her. She found herself going for long walks in the woods and trying to figure out how the craft she had seen stayed in the air. She would find herself in the old carriage house of the cloister where the handyman kept his tools. Slowly she started to learn how to use hand tools, and then she learned about machine tools and lathes, mills, and grinders.

The Mother Superior was concerned and spoke to her often about redirecting her thoughts to God's love and service. She would nod and speak quietly in German. Then she would head back out to tinker with an engine or motor. As the months had gone by, she found herself reading everything she could and thinking about the dedication of the teacher doing the research at the site where she had observed the object.

Then one afternoon, she saw an ad in a paper about a lecture being given in Boston. The man that was giving it was bearded and bespectacled. But the only thing for her that stood out in the ad were the letters *UFO's*. She had made arrangements to go to Boston and was hoping she would see someone that she knew from the investigation. But when she entered the hall, it was packed and she didn't recognize anyone in the crowd.

The speech had started out with an introduction, and then a heavy-set man in a tweed jacket stood and started to talk. Soon he was speaking so fast that the sister with her limited English could not follow all of his comments. But he was talking about visitations, landings, government cover-ups (she was not sure what those were), and the lack of people really trying to find out the truth.

The lecture was highlighted with slides and

drawings. At one point, he put up a drawing of a hovering spacecraft. It looked like the one she had seen in a small seacoast town in Massachusetts just a few months before. It was the same one that Sister Bernadette had seen on December 31. She felt a knot inside her throat and started to speak. Suddenly the lecturer stopped and looked at her.

"Do you wish to add something to this?" He glared at her as if she had done the unthinkable by interrupting him.

"Is...it...de...one...from...Massetooshuts?" She felt her face go warm as blood rushed into her cheeks.

"Massetooshuts? Sister do you speak English?" He pulled his pipe from his pocket and started to fumble with it. Someone on the stage spoke to him. He looked at his pipe, shrugged, and put it back into his pocket. He placed both hands on the lectern and leaned forward, waiting.

"Nein!...sprechen Sie Deutsche?" She didn't know what else to say.

"Of course I speak German, as well as French, Russian, Hindi, and four dialects of the upper Amazon, but I don't intend to use them in the middle of a lecture in New England —Jesus, Mary and Joseph! What I go through for thirty pieces of silver." He turned and walked back to the drawing. Suddenly he turned and broke into German.

"Have you seen one of these?" He pointed at the drawing on the stand.

"Yes, it was on New Year's Eve. It hovered for

nearly an hour then disappeared in a blur of light. It frightened a lot of the older sisters. They thought it was an omen."

"Superstitious balderdash. You would think in the later half of the twentieth century, we as a people would be smart enough to make every effort to commit complete genocide of poor twisted pagans, spending their days in quiet contemplation of some unknowable myth left over from a time when the human mind was totally incapable of looking at right angles without experiencing a complete schizophrenic collapse, for Christ's sake." He walked backed to the center of the stage and started to speak in English again. But before he had finished two complete sentences, the Sister spoke, this time a little more loudly and with conviction.

"Do you know how to take apart a Sterling Closed Cycle Engine and repair it? Or can you build one from pieces of metal just laying around the garage? I can. I can also get twenty-seven percent more horsepower out of it than anyone else, that is, by pressurizing the vessel with hydrogen." She was holding on to the silver cross that hung around her neck.

Mallory stood perfectly still for a moment. He looked across the audience and then back to the black-robed nun. People were quietly speaking to each other in expectation of his having her carried out of the hall. He pulled his pipe from the pocket of his tweed jacket, snapped his Zippo open, and lighted the toxic mixture of tobacco. Suddenly he broke back into German. "No one, not even God himself could get a twenty-seven percent improvement in a Sterling engine just by pressurizing it."

"Blasphemous heretic, may God have mercy on you," she retorted. "I did it by using a Rollsock seal on the power cylinder and on the hot side." She clung tighter to her crucifix.

"It worked?" He stood in the middle of the floor just looking at her.

"Better than I expected, but the heat exchange falls off at five hours." She realized the whole room was looking at her and trying to figure out what was going on between the nun and the bear-like lecturer.

"Have you worked with magnets or moving magnetic fields?" He pushed his notes aside and took out a pen.

"Yes, I have been able to sustain a fluxing field for over two hours, using carbon-boron magnets with a turning rate approaching fifteen thousand rpm." She wanted to run from the room. She had never made such a spectacle of herself, and if any of this got back to Mother Superior, she would be sent away again to someplace else. She knew she was too outspoken and proud, but she had learned all of this technical knowledge on her own and she was proud of it.

"Where in the blue blazes did you get carbon-boron magnets with any kind of power to do that?" The crowd was moving around, looking at their watches, wondering if this exchange would ever finish, and if this strange man would ever get back to his own presentation. He turned and looked at a middle-aged gentlemen in the front row who was acting out because he had paid to hear this lecture, not some discussion in a foreign language. Mallory turned and looked directly into his eyes. "Can you build and maintain a carbon-boron magnet that will hold a charge for over an hour, sir?"

The man tried to fold himself into a small tight package in the chair. He did not like to have all of this man's attention on him. He meekly responded, "Ah...well, no, I can't say that I could."

"Then just sit there and shut up until I am ready to reveal the secrets of the universe to you...." He looked back up at the sister and changed his tone. "Would you please wait after the lecture, so that we may speak a little more?"

She nodded and Mallory resumed talking about all the things that would fascinate the audience for an hour or so and then forget about.

When the lecture was over and the handshakes given, Mallory tucked the envelope that held the next month's worth of existence into his jacket pocket and made a straight line to the Sister. They walked out in the cold night air and stood by his car for an hour to exchange ideas on motive force. He asked her how she was getting back to the retirement home where she lived, and she told him that she would take the bus in the morning.

"No way!" he said, and before she could

complain about separation and the way things looked, he had tucked her into the front seat of the Dodge and they were speeding up the highway deep in conversation on energy exchange and magnets. That had started the relationship that had lasted for years, and which they shared in all parts of the world.

Ever since that day, whenever she would get a plane ticket in the mail and a card signed simply "M," she would make some lame excuse to her increasingly worried sisters and she was gone. Mallory was the only one who knew when she would return to the cloister and her normal way of life.

She now experienced a spark of excitement as she anticipated seeing the fascinating Dr. Mallory again. As she turned to the man at the base of the ferry ramp, her voice was soft and had that gentle charm of the Black Forest area of Germany. "Could you be so kind as to direct me to the local trolley, sir?"

Lindsey took in the complete vision in front of him. It seemed so out of place here. He had not remembered seeing a Catholic nun in Clover Bay since he had arrived here years earlier. He didn't even think that there was a Catholic Church in town. She was standing there smiling in her outfit that had always struck him as similar to the appearance of a penguin. There was a great crucifix hanging from her belt. He noticed the gold ring on her finger that carried the initials IHS. He had always wondered what that meant. He had also always wondered if nuns were bald under that great headpiece. He cut his speculation short and pulled himself together. "I'm sorry, Sister, but we don't have a trolley or bus service around." He thought for a moment and looked around to see if there was anyone else on the pier. It seemed deserted with the exception of the two of them.

"Oh, what a pity." She looked at the town and back to him.

"Perhaps I could offer you a ride to wherever it is that you are going." Clyde didn't really want to, but he felt that somehow the old adage about 'many are called but few are chosen' was at work right now.

"That would be wonderful." She started to turn.

"Let me assist you with your bags, Sister." Clyde reached for the larger of the cases.

"Oh, you probably shouldn't," she smiled a gentle smile. But still Clyde reached out and took the larger of the two cases.

With an impact like a supernova colliding into itself, the bag hit the pier with a solid thump. It took both his arms to pick it up, and he could feel the hernia forming in his intestines. When he tried to convey to her where the car was parked, his voice was little more than a choking whisper.

By the time they had crossed the hundred meters to the Dodge, Clyde was covered with sweat and hoped that wherever she was going did not have stairs. He knew that carrying this case would cause certain heart failure. It took two tries to get the larger bag into the rear of the car then he put the smaller bag in beside it. He opened the door to help her in, and made sure that all the folds of her gown were inside. He stumbled around the back to the other side. Harv was standing in front of the barber shop watching all this and noted to Lindsey, "Didn't know you were Catholic, Mr. Lindsey."

Clyde tried to reply, but there was only so much blood and energy in his body, and right then he needed every bit he had to get the door open and sit down to grab his breath.

"My, Sister, that is a heavy bag. Planning to stay awhile, I presume?" Lindsey fumbled with the ignition key.

"Those?" She turned and looked at the back of the station wagon. "Oh, no those are the tools of my trade. I brought the small case."

Lindsey thought to himself, "the tools of her trade?" It must be two thousand rulers, each with a thin metal strip running down one side to be used on erring knuckles!" He started the car and turned to her, "Where would you like to go, Sister?"

"My name is Maria Helen Diana Angelina Grossman from the Sisterhood of the Holy Order of Protection and Charity. But my friends just refer to me as Angel." She thrust out her hand to shake his. Her grip would have put Hulk Hogan on his knees.

"Well, Sister Angel...."

"Just Angel will be fine, kind sir. We are trying to be a little less formal these days since Vatican Two." She turned and straightened her robes. "I am looking for an old friend that said either he or one of his friends would be here to meet me. But it seems that he was being remiss, again." She looked around the small town and frowned. "End of nowhere is where this is, isn't it?"

"It's a nice quiet little burg," Lindsey offered apologetically.

"If you say so. I am here to visit an old friend, as I said, Dr. C. Thomas Mallory."

Within a millisecond, a medium in London by the name of Madam Sophia turned to the group of sitters in her salon and Carl Gustav Jung's voice was heard to yell, "synchronisity," to their wonder and confusion. A small nova on the other side of the galaxy imploded into itself causing a shock wave to travel outward that would not be felt on earth for some three thousand years. The center of Clyde Lindsey's head, somewhere near what the mystics call the Cave of the Brahma, exploded.

"Mallory sent me to pick you up, Sister." Lindsey sat back in the seat, felt what was left of his mind turn to mush and his frontal lobe ran away screaming.

"Oh!" She turned smiling. "So he is not the lying little prick that I thought he was a moment or so ago. Well good, let's be off and down the lane then, my dear. I have some good work to do here in this nasty little backwater of Protestant heretics."

Lindsey's mind ran quickly through what little history he had actually learned in college. The

Inquisition ended in the middle fifteen hundreds, did it not? The question hung in his mind, and then he started out of town toward the old Twitchell place.

Lindsey turned to Sister Angel with an inquiry. "Your English is a little strange, could it be a second language?"

"Why yes, the good doctor taught me in a summer period I spent with him in New England." She rolled the window down and let the cold air into the car. "He helped me to learn the language and its proper use." She sat there very smugly.

Lindsey decided just to let the matter go; if Mallory taught her English, it would not be proper. That is all that Lindsey knew about it.

WAYNE E. HALEY

CHAPTER 16

The whole group had been sitting around the parlor when they heard the Dodge pull up next to the porch. A shifting went through some of them and the others jumped up in anticipation.

Lighting a Camel, Ace commented, "Lord, let us be truly grateful for that which we are about to receive."

The door opened, and through it came a large gust of wind. Standing in the foyer was what some had referred to as the "nun from hell."

"All right, Mallory, you called and put up a red flare, and I am here. All I can say is that this better be really good 'cause if it isn't, Mallory, I'm putting you out in the streets of East Berlin on a wet Saturday night and pass the rumor you're the guy who designed the wall." She stood with her hands on her hips then turned slowly and saw Lindsey struggling with the large plastic case in the back of the station wagon. "Will somebody, for pity's sake, go help that poor fellow? He seems to have problems, especially with Temporal Discontinuity, did you know that, Mallory?"

"Oh yes, Sister, we know. And it is lovely as usual to see you, too — glad you're here." He threw his arms around her and gave her a great hug. "Tesla, please...." He pointed toward Lindsey.

Tesla came quickly down the stairs. Grabbing the bag with one hand, he sprinted back up the stairs and left Lindsey standing there with his mouth hanging open.

As Lindsey entered the room, he saw them all standing in a tight knot. He was trying to understand why they all knew each other so well. This, of all groups, seemed to be so disjointed and remote from any form of continuity or reality. Reality. The word lingered in his mind for awhile and rambled around like a large tumbleweed being carried in no particular direction by the wind. What exactly is reality? Was L.A. reality, or Clover Bay? A small smile started at the corner of his mouth and slowly spread across his face. The cat sat in front of him looking up at him. Those yellow eyes stared into his. "Hello, Haddoxes, how are you? You little sheep-stealing bastard."

All of those in the group stopped talking and turned to look at Lindsey. Then each turned and looked at Lady Lydia. She but shrugged. Lindsey walked up to where they all stood in the hallway and faced Mallory. "Since you seem to be the one running this home for the terminally bewildered, why have you brought us all together?"

"Us...!" Mallory exploded. He tossed his arms in every direction, pointing at the eight points of the compass with his pipe stem. In six languages and twelve seldom-used dialects, he mumbled nearly incoherent curses then blurted, "For Christ's sake. When did YOU, become one of US?"

"Before the first atom collided with the first meson. Before the word was uttered by proto man. When thought became reality and something or someone looked at his hand for the first time and decided that it contained as much of his soul as did his heart. When the nine Lords of Darkness descended the steps of the pyramid of Quetzalcoatl and carried the secrets of Ximballia back into the bowels of the earth, then it was decided." Lindsey reached over and took a Camel from Ace and tossed it into his own mouth. Ace lit it for him.

"Oh, I see...." Mallory was looking at him very carefully. "I think I know what's happened. It will be okay in awhile, when the side effects wear off."

Lady Lydia turned and started to walk back toward the kitchen. She glanced over her shoulder... "Want to bet?"

"That woman...," Mallory turned blue with anger. She was his own Ireana Adler, Helen of Troy, and Medusa all wrapped in one. And yet the qualities were beyond compare.

Clyde had walked out onto the front porch and seated himself on the steps. His head was swimming from the smoke and he felt the world go a little sideways. He had just begun remembering something about — the blackness filled the mind. He drifted into a calm current and rhythm that carried him into deep sleep.

Ace had walked up beside him and watched as Clyde fell against the banister of the steps. The banister was the only thing between Lindsey and a five-foot drop to the ground. The Camel still hung from his lips as his eyes rolled upward and he slumped sideways. Ace flicked the smoke away and with seemingly no effort at all, lifted the man into a fireman's carry, walked past the spectators in the front room and up the stairs to Margaret Twitchell's old room.

When Ace came back down, the assembly had moved into the parlor and was sitting in the large overstuffed chairs. They all stopped talking when Ace walked into the room and looked at him for some type of answer to the immediate question as to what had just occurred. He leaned on the doorframe and nodded toward Lady Lydia. "After effects, I would imagine."

With a shy smile she responded, "I would believe so. It does happen now and then. At least I've been told that by some."

"Yep, well, let's have a little powwow here and get down to business." Ace turned a chair around and sat on it backwards with his arms wrapped around the back. "Doc, you filled the Sister in on the scenario yet?"

"Was just getting to that, Ace, mostly just trying

to find out what's new and what Angel has been doing since last we met."

"Anything interesting, Sister?" Ace lit another smoke, but this time just to annoy her because he knew of her great dislike for smoking of any kind.

"Some, but we can run down that lane later. What is this story the Doctor here was telling last evening on the phone about you being all juicy over some saloon keeper?" Angel sat there with her best parochial-school-teacher look on her face — like she had just caught him in the boys' room with a girlie magazine.

"She is one hell of a nice girl, I will tell you...." Ace started only to be interrupted by Angel.

"And how would you know what a nice girl was, if my memory serves me correctly?"

"Hold on there, Angel. This is different. She is a nice girl and I have not tried, nor do I plan to try to corrupt this child." Again the "trust me" smile made an appearance.

"And if pigs could fly...."

"Angel, Ace. I didn't call this little conclave for you two to try to outdo each other in the depth and magnitude of verbal pugilism, which both of you are capable of. I would rather get back to my research, but Ace here believes that there is a problem and he has asked for some assistance. So...," with a venue of deference, Mallory turned to Angel, "...if you could forestall this verbal tirade until such time when the two of you can rip each other's hearts out without messing up the room or annoying the rest of us, could we please just put a lid on it?"

Everyone looked a little shocked at Mallory. "So blunt." The two words came from Lady Lydia and said so much.

"It's the climate, the weather, this attorney friend of yours, the fact that I can't use the scope enough to do a damn thing about that phase shift in the Typhien Expanse, Haddoxes and his sheep-stealing habits, Deputy Dimwit and his surveillance, and the fact that I came up here to get away from people and problems, and hoped that I could figure out what exactly was happening in or near that worm hole." Mallory puffed on his pipe.

"Darling," Lady Lydia's voice was soft and low, "of what importance is that worm hole in comparison to what Ace asked you about last night?"

"Well,...nothing, from one point of view. But equally, this is not a major problem, either, in the whole scheme of things in the spacio-temporal existence of consciousness in the universe. A single restaurant does not seem to need the collected power of this group to save it from probable extinction because a damn ferry is going to stop running." Mallory sat back feeling self-satisfied.

"Pard, it's not the fact that the restaurant closes and the ferry stops. It's the other way 'round. When the ferry stops, the restaurant won't make it. Then the bank will close it, and the little gal in there will lose seven years of bustin' her buns to give herself something worthwhile." Ace sat there, looking at the toes of his boots.

"So? It happens all the time." Mallory had picked up a computer printout and turned it over in his hands to check the backside for notes.

"Then why did you call last evening and ask me to be up at o'dark-thirty to get on that wreck of a ferry and come in such a hurry, Doctor?" Angel was boring a hole through him with her eyes.

"I'll get to that in awhile, but right now I want to know why I should spend time in this exercise." Suddenly there was a chill in the room as the two men's eyes met. The determination in each was as strong as the other's.

"All right," Ace said.

Lady Lydia finally interjected, "Is this some form of human male bonding that you two have to go through each time we solve some trivial problem? It seems like anytime one of you desires the other's help, you do this little dance about who is going to say it first."

"It's important," Mallory threw back.

"By all the saints, it's not. And you two need to stop playing Shut 'em Up at A.K Choral," Angel was playing with her rosary.

"Huh?" almost in unison came from three of the four people and the one face-shifter in the room.

"You know, that handsome tenor Burt Lancaster and Kirk whatever-his-name. The one that has the son with the girlfriend that puts rabbits in pots to boil without removing the fur. Oh, you know."

Haddoxes meowed twice in rapid succession. Ace and Lady Lydia turned to look at him. "Now what?" Mallory exploded.

"*Gunfight At The O.K. Corral.*" Both Lady Lydia and Ace turned at the same moment back to Mallory. It was Lady Lydia that said, "It seems to be one of Haddoxes's favorite movies also."

"All right, enough is enough. Forgive me, my friend." He turned to Ace and half-bowed in his chair. "But do tell me, what is so important about all this, and..." he raised his hand before anyone could speak, "I have already decided that I will do whatever I can to help. So, let's get past this quickly. Thanks be to Her Ladyship for showing me my errant ways, as usual." Mallory added with a small amount of sarcasm.

The discussion ran the gamut from what was happening about the ferry and the upcoming Council meeting to what Dixie Raye had said about the loss of the tourist trade and the net effect it would have on the town and more specifically on Dixie Raye's place. It was late in the afternoon and Lady Lydia had brought in sandwiches and coffee. The sun was descending across the water of Useless Bay, leaving an orange tint in the fog bank that lay on the water about four miles out. Ace had pulled the flask from his back pocket and laced his coffee. He passed the flask to Tesla who did the same. Mallory also. Then, upon passing it to Angel, she looked at Ace with her "you're-a-piece-of coyote-bait" look, crossed herself and then dumped two shots into her own coffee and passed the flask to Lady Lydia. She handed it back to Ace without using it. A shy smile passed between them.

"So what really chaps my hide, Doc, is the fact that this decision is being made without a hell of a lot of consideration for these folks here. Some little masturbating worm of a bean-counter is deciding that revenues are not high enough to keep this place from dying." Ace wiped the mayonnaise from his moustache. He looked up at Angel. "Sorry, it's just a form of speech from my part of the country."

She sipped her coffee and then looked up at him. "East Rusty Nut, Texas, probably."

The lights that Tesla had put on automatic timers clicked on around the room and also outside on the porch.

Mallory was in deep thought and suddenly the only sound in the room was that of the fans whirling in the computers that ran on the table under the window. There was also a distinct sound of someone snoring deep gulps of air upstairs. At this, Lady Lydia seemed to have that small smile return to her face. Mallory looked at her and asked quietly, "Is he going to be okay?"

"Never, but he will wake up in a couple of days or so. He needs all the rest he can get. Having that many neurons working all at once was an overload to his system," she gestured with her hands.

"Oh." Mallory wondered what the hell was in that drug she carried around with her.

That was something not even C. Thomas Mallory, Ph.D. was going to try. "You know, I think that you could put some permanent injury on some fellow — especially if he is out of shape."

Lady Lydia blushed and looked into her coffee. Angel crossed herself again and then turned to Mallory. "Leave her Ladyship alone. Different people, different customs."

"And you, the defender of the faith?" Mallory jested at her.

"That's the Priest's job. Remember they're the ones that defend the faith. We are only allowed to propagate the faith 'cause we don't have one of those thingies," at which everybody broke into laughter.

"Okay, so we need a plan to cause a change in the course of events. What would it take to convince someone not to stop the ferry and bypass this pristine little cesspool of civilization?" Mallory lit his pipe and puffed blue smoke into the air. His mind was a blank chalkboard that was starting to fill up with equations and probabilities.

"More people coming or wanting to come on that ferry." Ace had picked up another sandwich, lifting the bread to look at the substance between the slices. "Is this caviar?"

"Yes, it is," replied Lady Lydia.

"Didn't know they had this type in these parts."

"They don't." She sipped at her coffee. Both of them looked at Haddoxes, who was quietly chewing the end of Tesla's sandwich. Tesla sat on the floor next to the chair in which Haddoxes had perched.

"Oh...," Ace continued to eat.

Mallory's mind was someplace around the Saphirian Maelstrom by now, dealing with seven different dimensions of time and space. His eyes had glassed over and everyone just sat there waiting for his return.

WAYNE E. HALEY

CHAPTER 17

     In the final part of the last century, and the first part of this century, Edmund Husserl pushed philosophy to a new boundary, that being a field called "pure phenomenology." In his 1907 lectures in Gottingen, Germany he passed his original view as expressed in *Logische Untersuchungen*. He refuted Descartes and showed that logical thinking cannot end up in finding the final solution in the existence of God. Rather, each individual must look at all of life as a critical exam-ination not based upon presuppositions. Husserl pointed out that there are two types of "things" that exist in the world, those that are "outside" oneself and those that are "inside" oneself. By the use of pheno-menological reduction, all beliefs of "natural attitude" can be suspended.

     In short, all attitudes of common sense and science are disregarded, and all things that are not apodictic are removed. This, then, requires one to realize that all existence is internal and thought, or "pure thought" is the only reality in the entire universe. Everything outside the biological device called the brain and the process of eletro-chemical exchange within the neurofiber of tissue, which is abstractly called "mind," does not exist. It is only the representation which mind chooses to give to any natural object, condition, or event that truly matters.

All of this raced through Mallory's mind like sewage rumbling through the ancient pipes that crisscross the subterranean world of Paris. He pulled the scattered bits and pieces of himself back across the immense void of dimensional space and relocated them in the old white house on Wibley.

He looked at the faces that were looking at his. He took the old leather pouch from his jacket pocket and filled his briar pipe. He used his small silver pipe tool to work the tobacco deep into the recesses of the blackened socket, and then pulled the Zippo lighter from the other pocket. He read the Latin phrase that had been inscribed there so long ago. "Nos Locare Suis Haudquaquam." He looked at the man that had given the lighter to him after flying out of a shambles of an airstrip in the middle of the famine-ridden countryside of Afghanistan so many years before.

He considered for a moment that he and Ace had been together on so many last planes out. He rolled the small wheel over the miniature shaft of flint and the surface temperature rose to the point of combustion. The spark ignited the vapor of the petroleum fuel, which saturated the twisted cotton wick. The great flame that Prometheus died for flared into life. When contained, that flame warmed, fed, and protected ancient man from his fears of the night and terror that he held within his simple mind. But when allowed to run rampant, the fire could consume all that had taken hundreds or even thousands of years to grow or build. With the flick of that opposing thumb (the one that separates all primates from lesser mammals on this planet and in half the galaxy) the lid shut with its distinctive snap. With that snap came the diatribe of non-linear thoughts that had been gathered like sweet Kansas corn in September.

The blue smoke formed shapes as it rose from the end of the pipe. The shapes, whirling and dancing, twisted and collided noiselessly in the room. Mallory looked into each face and then down at his pipe. It sputtered and hissed on a large chuck of tobacco. "Well within the recorded history of man there have been only two ways that I know of to guarantee people will do exactly what you want them to do. The first is to scare the holy hell out of them," he turned to Sister Grossman, "nothing personal; the other is to provide them with a mystery for which they will go flat out, rat-ass crazy to find the answer. The first proposition is a little harder to do today, because if you threaten someone with excommunication or thermal nuclear war, and they call your bluff, you are suddenly in deep Kimchee to prove your point.

"It was much easier when people believed that

they had souls and that a Papal Decree would bar them from entrance into the Pearly Gates. Or when that Georgia peanut grower was walking around with Billy next to him, carrying the little black briefcase that could be used to obliterate the last five thousand years of earthly history.

"So, that kind of leaves us with providing a mystery — but not just any mystery. You can't bring in people because you have a mass-murderer working the neighborhood, or the curse of the pharaohs where everybody that touches the tomb of Mumbletyshit will die within six days and have the curse follow the family for the next six generations or until the Second Coming of Christ."

Lady Lydia raised her hand to cover her smile, Tesla looked blank, and Ace was smiling at Angel. Angel was twiddling with her rosary, a little more than before. Mallory wasn't noticing any of this, as his thoughts had filled the chalkboard to the point that it would require a buffer dump to get all the points out.

"So it has to be a mystery that will captivate the latent fantasy in the average, simple human primate mind. Something that will touch the child in each of us and allow us to believe in something that is greater than ourselves." He pointed his pipe stem at Ace. "Like forming a church. You have to offer something that nobody else has — you know like the 'name it, claim it' stuff the Charismatics are using now, or Babe Sees (or whatever his name is) with the ash falling out of his palms." He went back into his quiet reverie for a moment. "But one must be careful with religious mysteries."

"Wouldn't it have been a pleasant thing to have another Fatima right here in Cloverdale?" Angel asked.

"It's 'Clover Bay,'" Ace offered in his best and most cordial fashion.

"Oh, Clover Bay."

'Well, I had considered a similar idea, but then rejected it for several reasons. Primarily, there are difficulties between the faiths. If you have an appearance of some kind of figure of religious significance, then you have the true believers and then those that are of some other denomination that will try to prove that it's not the case. Historically, these events have gathered less and less spectators over the years. In 1916, in Spain, there were tens of thousands, but nobody beside the three kids saw anything. Interest waned and folks just kind of toddled off back home and went back to doing relatively unremarkable things.

"Today you could have the Second Coming of Christ, and if the Bears and Steelers were playing the same day on television, thirty people might show up to see the Son of God. About four hours later you would have the hatchet men from the Office of Special Inquiries, formerly known as the Inquisition, on your case, and anybody that was standing around would be convinced that they had not seen anything. So religious visions are probably a thing of the past."

"That is truly a shame." Perplexity crossed Angel's face.

"Maybe they will come back into vogue," Lady Lydia consoled.

"No, not in our lifetimes. I don't think so." Mallory was deep into his own thoughts by this time and everyone knew that it was better to just listen than do anything else. "So, that only really leaves two other types of occurrences that will bring a lot of people and a great deal of attention to this place in a short period of time. The first would be a monster sighting, but most of those are ripped up pretty quickly by biologists, and in these waters, everyone would buy into the 'decomposed whale' story really quick. Or the second choice, and the one that I believe will probably work, is that of a 'sighting.'"

Everyone looked at each other and then back at Mallory. "What sighting?" Ace asked.

"Why, the UFO over Useless Bay, of course. It has to be when all the people are together and able to corroborate each other's story real well. The witnesses must be local folks of unquestionable character, like 'Sleeping Beauty' upstairs, and it must happen at least three times in a period of two weeks. The same type of thing happened a couple of years ago down in Gulf Breeze, Florida. Had the place in an uproar for months. Made it on national television, and news services from all over the world came. Skeptics, too — by the droves. Must have pumped a million-and-a-half each month into the economy for at least seven months before somebody figured out that it was one enterprising guy and his handy-dandy video camera and a Frisbee with a cyalume lightstick attached." He was nodding his head up and down, indicating his internal conversation was as good as the external one.

"That's all well and good, but we would need to set up a hell of a video system to project an image out over the Bay that way," Ace suggested.

"That's the problem and Angel is the solution."

"What?"

"How?"

"Who?"

"See, the problem with most of these sightings is that they are limited to a few folks that can easily be discredited, and then the whole thing blows up. But if the sightings are made by lots and lots of folks, and then when the herd gets here to prove the locals have all contracted a case of St. Vidus Dance...Boom! You give them Act Two, Scene Three and right down to the water goes the ship, and it flies right across those high-speed Japanese-made cameras. When the roll of film is developed down at old Herb's Pharmacy, and everybody sees the damn thing then...," his eyes were wild with delight and he was standing waving his arms like Eugene Ormandy conducting the Philly.

"There is only one problem with your scheme," Lady Lydia waited for Mallory to regain control.

"What?" He tossed himself into his chair again and sucked on his pipe.

"You'll need a spaceship and if there was one, Haddoxes and I would be on it and gone before that intrepid band of spectators could show up. I know that this is a minor point, but since the whole plan is developed around it, I believe we are back to square one of the game."

"Wrong!" Mallory bellowed, "...your Ladyship, sorry, but wrong."

"How so?"

"We will build it. No, now, wait before you form the lynch mob. We are not going to build a real one of course, but a craft that can be flown above ground and have a high degree of maneuverability — something round and flyable. Quiet and quick." Mallory was fumbling through some notes.

"You're not talking about a Robertson Wasp are you?" Ace was leaning forward to the point of almost learning the same lesson that Margaret Twitchell learned about physics. "You wouldn't even think of one of those, would you?"

"Yeah, that's it...." Mallory pulled out a copy of the Robertson Flying Platform patent from the U.S. Patent Office. "It worked in the fifties and sixties really well. Heller bought up the patent and tried to peddle them to the Army as a single-person attack craft. But they didn't catch on for some reason."

"The reason is, people were getting themselves killed in them," Ace had retrieved some of his mass back into balance.

"A minor point. Bad workmanship, poor material, shit like that. Nothing we can't get past." Mallory handed the patent to Angel and then also handed her a drawing of an appended version. "And

Angel can build it."

"Sure and pigs can fly. But that thing is worse than a 'V-tail doctor killer.' Who in the hell do you think is going to fly that piece of junk if she can build it?" Ace hadn't noticed that everyone was looking directly at him. "Now, wait one goldarn minute here, if you think that I'm...."

"She is your girlfriend," Mallory offered.

"She's not my girlfriend. She's a nice gal, but no woman in the world is worth flying that hurling piece of shit for," he looked around for a moment — "present company excepted, of course."

"Of course," Lady Lydia said.

Tesla made a series of hand signs and pointed at Ace.

"What'd he say?"

"You don't want to know," Mallory intoned.

"What'd that half pint, slant-eyed little bastard call me?" Ace was standing.

"Doesn't matter," Mallory waved his hand. "It's so Zen, you wouldn't understand."

"What in the hell is that supposed to mean?" Ace was moving in a circle between the two men.

"It has to do with the fact that you started this conversation, but you're not man enough to..." Mallory was watching Tesla sign some more.

"Not man enough, you little pipsqueak? I'll show you 'man enough.'" Ace stopped as Mallory's hand went into the air, asking for silence. Tesla continued to sign very rapidly.

"He's right. By God, he is right." Mallory pulled out a pen and started to make some notes.

"Now you! You think I don't have the huevos to do it, after all we've been through together... I don't believe it." Ace was completely consumed by exasperation.

"No, it's not you. But Tesla just pointed out something really interesting that I had failed to grasp." Mallory was writing very quickly now.

"Well what the hell is this all about?" Ace had finally regained his control and sat back down.

"The Cult of Silence," Mallory said as he looked up.

"Oh, shit." Ace pulled a Camel and before he could light it, Lady Lydia took it from him and held it to her own mouth to be lighted by him.

"It would be just like when the Nazis, God curse their evil souls, came into Munich in '35. My Grandfather Henrick told me of those times." Angel was looking into the distant past.

"The little bastard's right. As soon as it looks real, they'll descend on this place like locust on a harvest," Ace interjected, remembering his dealings with the COS.

"Maybe we had just better forget the whole thing and go back to our research." Mallory turned to his computer and started to type.

"Hold on here, Doc," Ace said quietly. "We've had some dealings in the past with these folks and you have never backed down. They have cost you jobs, books not being published, a couple of wives — if my memory serves me correctly — and you never were real fond of them."

"True, but whenever the COS and the 'suits' from Washington show up, it normally means that everything is going to take a big dump on you." Mallory pointed to Lady Lydia and Haddoxes. "Plus, it's one thing to have Deputy Dimwit check up on us, but you want to expose our friends here to the COS, and have them try to figure out what happened to the sheep?"

WAYNE E. HALEY

CHAPTER 18

The morning returned to Clover Bay. The birds still chirped and the wind still blew gently out of the west. The trees still continued to turn autumn colors, and, on the surface, the world looked just about the same. But it wasn't.

Clyde Lindsey returned to what seemed like consciousness and found that he was still in Margaret Twitchell's old brass bed. He pulled the comforter up around his throat, looked into the morning, and wondered why he was still there. Ending up in this bed and in this house just had to stop. He was a man of responsibilities and had to get about them. After a shower, he dressed and descended the stairs to the parlor. It seemed as though the house was deserted. He poured himself a cup of coffee from the urn on the sideboard and started to munch on a Danish. He noticed from the ashtray that there must have been a long evening last night because the trays were overflowing. He also noticed that three of the smokes had lipstick on the ends. He walked over to the window and noted the knot of people standing beside one of the outbuildings.

He looked down at the yellow legal pad next to the computer that was still whirring away and read some innocent looking notes. One stood out and he did not know why. The words "The Cult of Silence" were scribbled there. Deep within his brain some vague reference made itself known to him. It was as if he had listened to a conversation about mysteries and reality and something to do with The Cult, but he could not pull it back to a high level of thought.

He mused over it for a few minutes and then saw a strange blonde woman in a black dress walking up to the house from the shop building. He knew her in some abstract way, but couldn't put his finger on it. She entered the parlor and looked at him with a warm smile.

"How are we feeling today?"

"Fine, I think," he stared at her for a moment, trying to remember the face and the unmistakable German accent.

"Good. It's good to see you back in the land of the living, saints preserve us." She walked past him, picked up a cup and filled it with coffee from the urn.

"We have met?"

"As sure as the Pope is Catholic — yesterday at the ferry dock. You brought me out here and then had sort of an attack. Poleaxed you right to the ground.

Must've been something that you ate." She picked up a Danish and put it back down again. "Angel," she pointed to herself, "came over from Seattle to see Doc." She watched him to see if there was any information flow going on inside his skull.

"Oh yes, Sister. Something about being called to see the good doctor and you had the traveling bag with dumbbells in it." He realized that it sounded stupid but it just came out that way.

"My tools, Mr. Lindsey, just my tools of the trade." She smiled and went back out the door, sipping her coffee reflectively.

He followed her down the steps still holding the coffee and the yellow pad. He strolled past the flagpole and looked up. "By God, there are three colors — all pink" he mumbled. With a shrug he followed Angel over to the shop.

Mallory, Ace, Tesla and Haddoxes were all standing around a set of plans laid out on the ground. The plans seemed hand drawn and crude. They seemed to be of a circular craft of some kind. Mallory was speaking to Ace while simultaneously signing to Tesla. They all went silent as Lindsey walked in behind Angel.

"Oh, you're still alive?" Mallory stuffed his pipe into his mouth and lit it.

"I shouldn't be?" Lindsey looked at all of them questioningly.

"Yeah, sure, why not? It is just a figure of speech, counselor. Now what can I do for you?" There was a moment of shuffling like small children caught behind the barn trying their first cigarette.

Lindsey raised the yellow pad and looked at it and then at Mallory. "What is 'The Cult of Silence,' it seems like I should know but the thought eludes me?"

Mallory noted the pad and then looked up to meet Lindsey's steady gaze. "Why would it seem familiar to you, counselor?"

"Oh, I don't know, but it comes in bits and pieces like a riddle that I have heard someplace. I heard somebody talk about it once, perhaps. It's just that it rang a bell or two in my mind." Lindsey was staring at the pad again when Lady Lydia walked into the shop in a black jumpsuit. She looked at Mallory, Lindsey, the pad, and the others.

"Hyper Sensory Awareness caused by neuro-transmitter reconstruction. He heard everything you said last night, even while he was asleep." She picked up Haddoxes and started to rub him gently.

"Uh,...well listen, counselor, I'll tell you about it later, but right now I need some questions answered. Let's take a walk." Mallory put an arm through Lindsey's and moved him down the path toward the beach.

"It's okay. We'll start without you, Doc." Ace was wearing his Evel Knievel grin and went back to the drawing. "Is 'asshole' a hyphenated word or not?" he asked over his shoulder.

"What's going on, Doc? Are you putting together a small sacrifice or just preparing for World War Three?" Lindsey was staring back at the knot of people talking and pointing at the drawing.

"That's about it, counselor, but let me ask you, how do you feel?" Mallory had herded him toward the beachfront.

"Mostly with my hands," Lindsey said with the beginning of a grin. He noticed the seabirds sitting on the beach and the way they clustered around in groups. He had not noticed that before, ever. "They seem to be socially dependent creatures, wouldn't you say, Doc?"

For a fleeting moment, Mallory looked puzzled. "Them?" He pointed with the stem of his pipe back toward the shop.

"No, the birds. Have you ever noticed that no sky hunters are social in their makeup? Those birds that are predators are solitary in their fashion." Lindsey was enjoying the morning. It was slightly gray and yet felt warm to him.

"On occasion, I have noticed that fact. In fact, I wrote a paper on it about twelve years ago for a nature magazine." He played with his pipe trying to get the last remaining bits and pieces of tar and tobacco out of it.

"I must have read that, then. It seems familiar to me." Lindsey looked at the distant skyline and could see some of Clover Bay through the foliage.

"Doubt that, they never published it. Said it was too psychological for them." He started to fill his pipe again.

"Doesn't matter." Lindsey turned and looked

into his own image in the glasses that Mallory was wearing. "What's up, Doc?"

Mallory stood transfixed, his thoughts were a jumble between not knowing whether to be angry or to laugh. "Well, counselor, I need to ask you a question of some importance. Basically, is there any upcoming event at which the whole community gets together in our small burg of ignorance?"

Lindsey was studying the bobbing movements of the birds as they waddled around each other. "Normally, most of the major events are through. They finish at the end of summer, so I don't think that there will be anything until next year." He pointed toward the white gulls near the water's edge. "They say that sea gulls are the incarnated souls of sailors lost at sea. Did you know that?"

"Yes. But is there nothing that the town gets together for, like a church social or potluck? Anything?"

"Normally, they would have the cranberry picking, but since you bought the only place with fields, nobody expects that to happen this year. Margaret would normally open the fields on a Sunday and let everyone come over and pick their fill. Then there would be a potluck here. But that doesn't seem to fit anymore." Lindsey fished a piece of gum out of his pocket, unwrapped it slowly and popped it into his mouth. "Interesting the way we make food that has no nutritional value."

"When?"

"When what?"

"The cranberry pick."

"Usually during the first couple of weeks in November."

"Good. Two weeks. Will you tell everybody that the second Sunday of November we will have a potluck and open the fields for them?" Lindsey looked questioningly.

"Sure, if you will tell me about 'The Cult of Silence.'" Lindsey took the gum from his mouth and looked at it. "Must have a lot of sugar in it 'cause it stings the back of my throat."

"Good, in two weeks."

"If you tell me about The Cult of Silence. If not, the whole little thing will become gossip in the local weekly." Lindsey turned and looked directly at Mallory who was thunderstruck.

"Blackmail, counselor? Is this what it has become? And what exactly would you tell the local rag?" Mallory suddenly regained his composure and stood there with that blank stare of an evangelist gone bad.

"Let's begin with the fact that you are conducting research on time/space distortions, using Einstein's Tensor Equations. Secondly, that you have contact with alien life forms from a remote star system. Thirdly, that you have penetrated certain classified and confidential, to say the least, files using your positions at various colleges, and have collected enough secret information to make the Rosenbergs look like amateurs. Now, in truth, that may be laying it on a little heavy, but imagine when Deputy Dimwit reads it. He'll start the next phase of the 'mother of all investigations' to coin a phrase." Lindsey stood in the morning light and enjoyed the sounds and movement around and across the Bay.

Mallory stood there just looking at Lindsey's profile. "God, how I wish she would not use that truth-sayer drug." Muttering and grumbling to himself, he headed back toward the shop. With his arms tossed out, it appeared as if he were talking to someone else.

CHAPTER 19

Lindsey was looking out of the window that overlooked Useless Bay. He had been staring at the boats that were moored there for at least an hour when the door opened and Harv came in. He stood there for a few minutes and then cleared his throat in a loud sort of way. "Mr. Lindsey?" "Mr. Lindsey?"

His reverie broken, Clyde glanced up to see Harv standing in the doorway. "Yes, Harv, what can I do for you?"

"Is it true that we can go over to the old Twitchell place next Sunday and pick berries?" Harv was holding a piece of colored paper. Lindsey got up and looked at it. It was a simple notice of a cranberry picking party and potluck dinner over at the old Twitchell place on the following Sunday, and it was signed by himself as Mallory's representative.

"It's just that the wife wants to know if this is true or some kind of joke, 'cause if it's true, then she needs to pick up sugar and Certo for the jelly making. Then she needs to call her girlfriend and figure out what she should bring for the potluck. She tells me that it would seem strange that this here doctor would do something like this, but I sorta told her that you had a hand in it and that made it okay." Harv stood there waiting for a response, something akin to Travis's waiting in the Alamo.

"It's true, Harv." Lindsey sat back down and tried to think of what Certo was and why anybody would want it.

"Oh, okay." Harv just turned and walked back to the barbershop and left Lindsey to his own thoughts.

Clyde Lindsey had bits and pieces of information floating through his head like so much flotsam and jetsam, but nothing seemed to make much sense. He picked up the phone and called information. The disembodied voice at the other end asked, "What city?"

"What is today, please, the date and day?"

"November·first, what city please?"

He hung up the phone and looked at the calendar on his desk. The date staring back at him was six-days old. Where had he been and what had he been doing?

One of the flyers concerning the cranberry pick and potluck was sitting on his desk. He looked at it and then walked over to his Xerox machine and pulled the paper-feed tray out. Blank paper of the same color was in the feed tray. He then rewound his answering machine and listened to the messages. Most were the same old stuff he had heard before with the exception of duplicates and people asking him why he did not return their calls in a more timely manner. Then he heard the voice of doom on his tape. This small piece of plastic that had been imprinted with metal particles had received the electromagnetic distortions which, when amplified, modulated a sound that seemed to replicate a human voice in both tone and timbre. "Lindsey, when you get this message, call me and I will explain. This is Doc."

What had gone on for the last six days? He was completely lost, and yet there were bits of information that rolled and moved through his head. He must have been back here he thought, for there was mail on his desk, some of it postmarked within the last three days here in Clover Bay. He sat back down and started to think about making a medical appointment to check out the possibility of him having...what was it they had said? ...PPD with discontinuity. He wondered if there was a treatment for it or not.

He thumbed through the Rolodex on his desk and then decided that he would rather have something to eat than to see another doctor. He strolled down the sidewalk and spoke to a couple of townfolks, but for the life of him could not remember their names. He walked into Dixie Raye's. She was just putting some plates down between two people from Tacoma. "Take your usual seat in the corner booth, Clyde, and I'll get your lunch." She disappeared into the back of the restaurant and he heard some voices speaking.

Clyde Lindsey looked out onto the Bay and wondered where the last few days had gone. "Cranberry Pick at Mallory's?" He spoke to the empty air on the other side of the booth. He had produced the flyers, but for the life of him he simply could not remember doing it.

"There you go, just like you like it. Chicken fried steak with extra gravy." She also set down a glass of diet soda next to his plate. "Things have improved since I got that new cook. Everybody just seems to love the way he puts stuff together." She was off to talk to someone else who had just come in from the street.

He looked at the white gravy ladled over the meat and wondered why she had told him this was his favorite meal. He didn't remember ever eating a chicken fried steak before. He had always been a poached fish eater. And never gravy. It was too high in cholesterol. He found himself digging into it and telling himself that this was not his favorite meal, but within minutes he had devoured the entire contents of his plate and was wiping his mouth on the linen napkin. About then, he felt a looming presence over his shoulder and glanced up to see the grinning face of Ace looking down at him.

"How ya feeling, Clyde?" Ace sat down across from him.

"I'm not sure."

"That's to be expected after what you have been through and all. It's not easy to spend that much time

listenin' to Doc and not have some major side effects."
Ace lit up a smoke and pushed the pack across to
Lindsey.

"I don't smoke." Lindsey had pulled one of the
Camels out of the pack and used Ace's Zippo to light
it.

"Yep, I know you don't." Ace put the pack back
into his white shirt pocket. "You know that you look
like a deer caught on the road at night in somebody's
headlights!"

"It's funny, I feel like I suddenly know a lot
about a lot of things, but I can't seem to pull them up.
They're just floating there and I don't know what to
do with them." There was a spot of white gravy
clinging to the edge of his mouth. Ace handed him a
clean napkin and pointed.

"Oh, sorry." He felt embarrassed at both the
gesture and the comment.

"Don't be. It's new ground, the undiscovered
territory, the future that you have come up against and
most people are not ready to deal with it or even
understand it very well." Ace turned halfway around
and looked out at the Bay. "I love water, any kind of
water. From cobalt blue of the tropics to gray-white
of a stormin' northern maelstrom."

"I really never noticed it much until lately. Now
it seems to have become part of my existence." Clyde
drank half of a cup of coffee in one pull. "Tell me what
Doc meant by 'The Cult of Silence'?"

"Oh, I don't know, counselor, if that is a good

idea or not. Maybe...."

Lindsey cut him off abruptly. "Come on, Ace, for Christ's sake, I probably won't remember it past this afternoon. I am forgetting more and more all the time." He motioned to the flyer about the cranberry picking party set for Sunday.

Ace got a far-off look in his eyes, like he was trying to either remember or forget something. He crushed out his smoke and started to doodle with his pencil on the flyer that lay between them. "It started back about '43 in the summer. Some guys from the Navy Department had come up with an idea about how to screw up the surface radar that the Nazis used to find our convoys. It seemed like Von Neuman, Einstein, and a guy by the name of T. Townsend Brown had gotten together. They came up with this idea that if they put a toroidal magnet around a ship and energized it with high frequency and high potential electricity that it would create a sorta electronic fog. It would allow the ship to move around freely without anybody's radar seeing it. They used a new destroyer called the Eldridge. It wasn't commissioned yet, so nobody would really notice the ship missing. They spent about three weeks hooking the system up and working on it at the Philadelphia Naval Yard. Some time in July they took her out of the harbor and zapped 'er."

"Okay, so they were working on a stealth system right?"

"Yep, but there was only one problem. When

they threw the switch, the ship became invisible all right, but not for the reason they thought. The ship was suddenly in Norfolk Harbor — about five hundred miles away. They had moved the ship through space and time. They hit the switch again and the ship went back to the same spot it was in at Philly. The crew was left completely messed up. A dozen or so sailors went stark raving mad. A bunch more were so radiated that they would be in the hospital for years, and some of them had completely vanished off the face of this earth. Einstein went back to Princeton and burned all of his notes on Tensor Equations, Brown had a nervous breakdown, and Von Neuman was packed up and shipped off to some highly classified laboratory for the next thirty years to see if he could replicate the experiment." Ace lit another Camel.

"So?"

"That's when it started."

"What started?"

"The Cult of Silence." Ace looked around the restaurant and noticed nothing out of the ordinary. "After that, a lot of things started happening and nobody really knew how to explain them. Within a few years, the sky was filled with UFOs. Everybody was seeing them and a lot a people started to do research into what they were and where they came from. Then a lid got dropped on everyone. One by one, a lot of hard working folks that were looking for answers got shut up. Guys would show up and tell them...God knows what they told them. But folks that had spent years trying to find out answers about UFOs were suddenly working on raising roses and making birdhouses."

"This sounds like a conspiracy theory to me. Is that where this is leading?" Lindsey walked over to the coffee maker, poured himself another cup, filled one for Ace and brought them back to the table.

"That is what they want everyone to think. Anybody that starts to make noise is either shut up or branded a wacko of some kind and is totally discredited."

"What purpose does that serve? Sure, if there are saucers out there, it makes sense that the government isn't going to say anything. Theorists have projected stock market failures, religious wars and just plain folks doing an Orson Wells number and killing themselves because the end is near. Now, it would be tough for the government to say anything because it has been so long. Oh, yeah, by the way, we have known about this for forty years but we had more important fish to fry." Lindsey sat back in the booth and eyed Ace with his best "disapproving lawyer" stare.

"Sure, if it were that simple." Ace drew a rough map of the U.S. on the back of the flyer. "Here's Philly, here's D.C. During the ten years after the experiment, the skies are littered with craft. The Air Force is trying to find out something, and suddenly...boom! They shut down. Nobody in the government can talk to anybody about this. Why?"

"There are ample studies. I remember in college

a Doctor from Utah headed up a complete scientific study and found no evidence about UFOs at all." Lindsey found a small irritation growing in the center of his mind.

"Sure, Condon and the group of other bozos were hired to discredit the study. It was easy to do. But the problem was that everybody who knew about the study was silenced, so nobody came forward. That is when Doc started to take an interest in it. It was too clean, too perfect. 'Nope, nothing there, boys, so let's get on with business.' But it didn't make any sense, that is until he found out that what started at Philly had continued. But...not in the direction people might expect. These guys were trying to replicate the experiment at places like Montage, New York and Fallon, Nevada. They were trying to plug up a mistake.

"When the Eldridge was zapped, it ripped a hole in the fabric of space. Somebody or some*thing* from a different place happened to bump into it and suddenly found themselves here in survival mode. The last forty years have seen nothing but the government of this country and five others trying like hell to close an electromagnetic doorway that the Eldridge opened in '43. It moves from spot to spot around the earth and works at different phases and times, but it keeps showing up."

Lindsey was leaning across the cafe table and listening very carefully now. "What are you saying — exactly?"

"The gateway is out of control. They, that is

'The Cult,' aren't trying to build time machines or conduct experiments about moving objects through space and time. They are bleeding huge drops trying to close this rip in space before something comes through that neither they nor anyone else can explain away. You know, something like an entire landing force of 'things' from Beta Zetta Four."

Lindsey sat transfixed and looked out at the moving water for what seemed like an hour, yet it was slightly under a minute. He had started to sort facts and ideas and draw certain conclusions.

"My God!"

"Yep."

"That's why the computers, the scope, and..."

"Figure something out, counselor?" Ace sat back and crossed his arms waiting for Clyde to return to that point referred to by mystics as the ever-present now.

"Lady Lydia of the Stygian Triangle...that's not a joke, is it, Ace?"

"Let me give you the rest, Clyde. For the past ten years, this country has been hyping the SDI (Strategic Defense Initiative) to everybody as a defense tool against the Russians. But in reality it is a highly sophisticated locating, tracking, and identification system. It's designed to find that open doorway and then hit it with high energy particle beams in the belief that they can close it back up.

"The only problems are that the Russians went into Chapter 11, and that Doc figured out that if one pulses the gateway with a high charge of pure electrons, it will not close the doorway but rather tear it open even wider."

"Sitting with the hired help, Mr. Lindsey?"

It took Clyde a second to deflect from the story that Ace was revealing and look at the chubby ferret-like man standing by the table. Deputy Bob was leering down with his thumbs wrapped around his Sam Brown Belt. Looking from one man to the other and back again Bob said, "Just concerned 'cause nobody seems to have seen you or heard from you in awhile."

"Last time I checked, Deputy, it was still a free country and people could come and go as they wished." Lindsey took another one of Ace's cigarettes and lit it.

"Well, maybe that's true, but...."

"Deputy. It is true, and now find something else to do besides bothering us."

"Just concerned and doing my duty." The deputy walked off and found a stool at the counter where Dixie Raye had been patiently keeping her distance from the two men next to the front bay window. She filled up a cup of coffee, put it down next to the deputy and walked back into the recesses of the kitchen without a word.

"Does Ms. Russell know anything about this?" Lindsey leaned over the table to keep his voice low.

"No, and she doesn't know about the reason for the cranberry pick, either." Ace, too, was leaning across the table.

"How does the cranberry pick and SDI fit

together?" Lindsey found that some bits and pieces were still missing in his mind.

"You'll find out, counselor, in good time, but right now we need your help to get as many folks out there as possible on Sunday, and just have them pick away at those little beggars." Ace's 'trust me' smile had returned.

"Why do I feel I am part of a conspiracy?"

"'Cause it was your idea." Ace got up and walked back into the kitchen.

About the same time, Dixie Raye wandered back out with a fresh pot of coffee to refill Clyde's cup. "Ain't he something? Didn't know that you and Ace were so close." She stood there holding the Farmers Brother Pyrex coffeepot and looking down at Lindsey with a strange far-off shadow on her face.

"It seems like I have known him all my adult life, Dixie, yet just found that fact out." He smiled up at her and felt a genuine sense of warmth for the woman. "How is it all going for you?"

"It's still okay, but after that damn ferry hearing, I'll probably be either learning how to fill out forms for the county or buying a bus ticket to Idaho. It just doesn't seem right, somehow." There was a degree of forlornness in her voice. "In some ways," she said, glancing around her world, "it seems like this has been a lot of work for nothing."

"I wouldn't worry about it too much, Dixie. Things have a strange way of changing from day to day." He sipped his coffee and found that he was truly enjoying it.

"Do you really think so? I don't know how, but then I'm just a hash slinger. I know that you're involved in all those negotiations with the county and ferryboat company, but still...." She drifted away back toward the kitchen.

•••••

The sky was electric blue over both Useless Bay and inside Lindsey's mind. He felt that he could reframe his thoughts in a distinct way that he had never been able to do before. The pulsing of the neurons was evident to the microscopic level in him, and he was working through possibilities faster than he had ever thought imaginable. He sat there for several minutes lost in thought, when at last the whole universe fell into view for him. He sat back. His eyes opened in wonderment at his own ability to process a myriad of information in such rapid succession. He muttered to himself, "Of course! That is the only way." He got up and walked back toward the swinging kitchen door and strolled right on in. Ace was cutting vegetables and putting them into a pot for soup. Dixie was wiping down the chrome worktable with a white dishcloth. She looked up as he pushed through the door and leaned on the counter next to her.

"Is there something wrong?" she asked, puzzled.

"No," he thought through the words carefully,

"but I want you to hear some of the best advice that any lawyer could ever give you. And I am going to give it to you absolutely free, which must violate at least three canons of the ABA code of ethics. Over the next few weeks, there are going to be a lot of folks showing up here in town, and some of them are going to be looking to buy things. A few of them are probably going to talk to you about this place."

"Why is that, Clyde? What would be the reason?" She looked perplexed.

"The reason? Let's just say that I have a hunch. If I'm right, somebody will offer you a lot of money for this business." He looked directly into her blue eyes. "Sell it, Dixie. Take the money. Put it into an account in Seattle or Portland, not here. But take the money and run."

"Yep," Ace agreed while still working on the vegetables. He didn't look up.

"But why? If people are going to be here, shouldn't I...well, it would seem like...," she felt the confusion in her growing.

"No. You should sell this place for the best price you can and then figure out where you would like to go." Lindsey turned without further comment and walked out.

Deputy Bob turned and started to say something, but Lindsey walked right past him and out into the cool air. He knew and suddenly knew that he knew.

CHAPTER 20

Lindsey had walked back to his office and looked toward his desk. They were there, just as he knew that they would be. The keys.

He went out the back door, not taking time to lock the door, and straight to the green '50 Dodge station wagon parked under the carport. He got into the car, opened the glove box, pulled out a cassette tape of the Grateful Dead, and slammed it into the gaping hole of the player. He twisted the key in the ignition and started the engine with a push of the starter button. Easing out of his driveway much the same way that Mario Andretti eases past the green flag at Indianapolis, he exploded down the main street with Jerry Garcia ripping at strings filling his ears. Opening the ashtray, he found a perfect set of rolled joints and lit one up. He started to speak to the openness of the Bay on his left. "I knew Pigpen before Southern Comfort got his liver...but I just forgot for awhile who

I IS…boy, howdy!"

He felt the purring of the machine under his hands as he hit seventy down the old Bay Road. "God, I love this car. This was built when people knew how to build real things, before plastics, worries about cholesterol, tofu, and jerks running for president." He noticed two Indians walking back up Bay Road. They were carrying some bags of groceries that they had bought in Clover Bay and were returning to the reservation. He slammed on the brakes and skidded to a stop. Flinging the door wide open, he greeted them. "Yuttahay!"

The two natives looked at the plume of smoke coming from the car and then looked at the driver and back at one another.

"That's Navajo, isn't it?" one of the men said to the other.

"It's all I know. Want a ride back up the road?" Lindsey turned Jerry Garcia down to a dull roar.

"You're the attorney in town. Why?" One of the men was leaning down to look into Lindsey's face.

"Because I was too stupid to study something worthwhile or learn a trade, that's why."

"Oh. Okay." Both men piled into the backseat with their bags, then with a roar of the engine Lindsey floored it again.

He passed them the joint. Both took a hit and handed it back. "Good smoke." The music blared.

He propelled the car down the old reservation road, went right past the chapter house that marked the outside boundary of the reservation, and indicated in the air for one of the men to tell him where to go. One pointed to an old yellow and white mobile home sitting among the trees. A small fishing boat on a trailer sat in the front yard. He pulled up in front of the trailer, switched off the engine and let the Dead finish their song. Then he jumped out, opened the door and helped the older man with his bags. The man was giving him a strange look like he was from the government and he was "here to help them."

"I'm Lothak and this is my son Michael." The older man nodded with his chin to the younger. "A Christian name that folks told me would help him to get a job. But it didn't."

"You fellows salmon fishermen?"

The old man looked at the younger and then back to Lindsey. "Why?"

"I might have need of a couple of good fishermen starting this Sunday." Lindsey passed the joint back to the older man who took it and passed it to his son.

"Salmon's bad this time of year, go farther south into Oregon. Not many in the Bay." The old man pulled a Budweiser from the bag, held it for a moment and then handed it to Lindsey. "Against the law for an Indian to have alcohol on the reservation."

Lindsey popped the top and took a gulp, "Yep. Listen, I want you two to look like you're fishing for maybe half a day or so out on the Bay. It's worth a couple of hundred — each."

"Each?" The younger man could talk.

"Yeah, but it's got to be between us. Let's just say that it's lawyer business."

"Like the guys that fight the insurance company and win a lot of money for the white girl that has the neck brace in the ad on television?" The older man took the joint back and smoked deeper on it.

"Something like that…you game?"

"When and where?"

"I will tell you in a few days. Get your boat ready and I'll be back to talk to you, okay?" Lindsey turned to get back in the car and the older man held out the joint to him. "Keep it. I'll see you soon. Oh, by the way," he pulled out his billfold, took out two twenty-dollar bills and handed one to each man. "A retainer for your services."

Both men blinked, looked at the money and then back to Lindsey. "See ya."

CHAPTER 21

Mallory had been running back and forth between the house and the shop all morning. It seemed as though everything was going well, but he just wasn't sure all his calculations were correct, the conjunction of the two efforts would be close and timing was all that mattered. He had been puffing on his pipe so much that the inside of his mouth felt like the Korean Army had marched through it with muddy boots. He sat by the three computers and ran another series of scans. It was there, still working, and seemed to be on track. He wondered if those geeks at Hemispherical Defense Command had detected the pattern yet. Probably not. They were too reactionary to use enough insight to figure out what tomorrow held, let alone what might occur two weeks from today.

Doc turned to find Lady Lydia standing there holding a tray of coffee and sandwiches. "You need to eat something. It has been two days since you ate or slept. You need your strength." She sat down beside him.

"Time, Your Ladyship? I never have enough time to get it all done, and now with this added component, well...." He pulled hard on his pipe and filled the room with blue smoke.

"This added component is what it is all about, in reality. Is it not?" She was smiling softly at him.

"Perhaps, but it seems that doing the research is one thing, but using it for such a low purpose seems to elude me. I have, perhaps, spent too much time in the lofty halls of theory. I must be the first to admit that I miss the human aspect, sometimes. That is probably the reason I am surrounded by such truly human friends to remind me...," he paused and looked at her carefully, "...no insult intended."

"None taken. It is just that you look at life, no matter where it originated, as human. It is a complex thought that would allow you to alter the word. For the most part, it is really unnecessary since 'human' conveys the point so well." She stood and straightened her jumpsuit, which seemed to fit as though it was sprayed on. "Eat something and take the two red pills. They will help keep you going."

"Ah," he looked at the two globes lying next to his coffee cup.

"No!" she smiled, "they're not those kind of pills. Just some neuro-transmitter enhancer that will allow you to continue without sleep for another few hours. And they have no side effects."

"Oh," he took them without further questions. She left the room and he finished a sandwich and then resumed his work at a keyboard.

He heard the gate open and saw the car drive up next to the house. "Great! The Clarence Darrow of Clover Bay is back. More 'fun with learning' is about to descend upon this house for the terminally bewildered." He refilled his pipe and fished for the Zippo lighter in his tweed jacket.

Haddoxes walked into the living room, jumped up by the computers and stared at the screens, his yellow eyes intent. He turned and looked at Mallory and meowed three times.

"I know, but here we have the counselor who is about to ask more inane questions about why and what and when Caesar crossed the Rubicon. Oh, well. The little trials that we must all go through, my friend." He looked at the cat again. "Don't worry. It's just a figure of speech, you sheep thief."

With that, Haddoxes jumped down and strolled over to the overstuffed chair. He curled up in it and watched the doorway. Lindsey walked in, reached down to rub the cat and play with it for a moment.

He sauntered over and looked at a display screen on one of the computers. He picked up Mallory's coffee cup and sat down facing the man who had a permanent pipe stuck in his mouth.

"I got us a couple of Indians to be out on the Bay on Sunday and told them to look like they're fishing. That way, if Ace has to ditch, somebody will be there who can pick him up and nobody will be the wiser. Secondly, it would seem that Tesla should add some kind of explosive charge to the Wasp in case it does go down. There shouldn't be a trace of it left for 'The Cult' to find. Thirdly, you're going to need some-body from the media to get the story. Any ideas?" He sipped at Mallory's coffee and looked at the older man who stared back at him, transfixed.

"On the second run, this place should be filled with journalists. Now, what gave you the idea that you knew what was going on?" Mallory was dumbfounded.

"Second run. Makes sense. Lends more credibility to the sighting, and by then the Feds should have figured out that the electromagnetic window is open. Listen. What if you get a real phase shift and a couple of crafts come through at that time?" Lindsey leaned forward in the chair, anticipating the answer.

"Let's hope so. That will take some of the heat off of us, and allow us to add the window dressing necessary. Now, just how has all of this come into your purview, might I ask?" Mallory offered him a sandwich that Lindsey took even though he was not hungry. It was caviar and it tasted good.

"Simple reasoning. Rule out all that could not occur, and whatever is left is the way it's got to be. Simple deductive reasoning, I would say. It is so simple; I am surprised that nobody else has figured it out. Except knowing the average intelligence of the human species, it is not surprising that few people even know what is happening around them. Jesus, if you believe those clowns in Washington, they would make you think that everything is all right and tomorrow holds great promise for all of us." Lindsey finished the sandwich between pauses in his diatribe and refilled the cup. "How are Angel and Tesla doing?"

"He claims she signs with an accent and that she is nothing more than a garage repair person, where he is pushing the limits of engineering. She claims that he is a true example of an oriental — inscrutable in thought, word, and deed. She knows that he is truly a pagan at heart and if he would only embrace the cross, he would be a much better Jap. In all, they are doing fine. Some minor problems, but nothing that they can't work out. But what is all of this to you?" Mallory realized that he was answering questions more than he was asking them. This was strange and out of context for him.

"Well, if our plan is to work...," Lindsey started.

"OUR plan! Jesus, Mary and Joseph. When did this become 'OUR' plan?" Mallory exploded and started to pace the room, pointing his pipe in a hundred directions at the same time and swearing in three African dialects.

"It became our plan when you walked into my office. You knew that then, and now so do I. So, don't look so surprised. And by the way, this is not your normal way of getting converts to your faith, is it, Doc?" Lindsey walked over and rubbed Haddoxes's belly and the cat rolled over and started to play. "Can and will you teach me how to understand Haddoxes's language?"

"Yes and probably. If we have time. Now, counselor, if you wouldn't mind, I have work to do. And so do you. Get the word out that people really need to be here."

"Done. By the way, is Lydia around?" Lindsey looked around the room and down the hall. "Upstairs, but don't take any more of her funny pills. At least not right now. I do think you would be better off keeping a clear head for the next few days." Mallory sat back down at the terminals and started to type in something else.

"Done, Boss." He strolled out and up the stairs.

CHAPTER 22

The night had been another success at Dixie Raye's diner. A portion of the success was due to her new cook. He had taken the same old ingredients, but had put them together in new and unusual ways that delighted the pallet of many of those in and around Clover Bay. Once again the place had been filled to capacity on this wet autumn evening. Salmon, poached with a white cream sauce, had been accented by small mounds of potato puffs garnished with parsley. The French onion soup had been such a big success that many of the locals had asked for the recipe. Ace had provided it courtesy of Clyde's copy machine.

As the last local left and Dixie Raye closed and locked the door, she tossed herself into one of the booths and unsnapped her barrette. She shook her hair loose and sat back exhausted. "God, if it keeps up like this there is no telling what will become of this diner."

Ace walked over, put two cups of coffee down, and lit his smoke. She reached across and took it, pulled a drag off it, and handed it back. "Swore I would never do that."

"And you shouldn't. It will stunt your growth." He sipped his coffee.

"As if you noticed. The only thing I haven't done is stripped naked, thrown myself on top of a table and screamed 'do me!' But then, I think you would tell me there was something else that needed 'do'-ing in the kitchen." She pulled at her blouse. "'Course, no one would blame you because I smell like a sheep that has been out in the pasture too long."

"You look fine, smell fine, and are fine. It's just that everything has a proper time and this is not it." He walked over and poured two more cups of coffee. "But it will be soon."

"Promises, promises," she toyed with her hair. "Are you like the old Flying Dutchman? You heave-to into a port for awhile, then drift away some night like smoke from a fire, never to be heard of or seen again?"

"No," he laughed. "No, not at all. It's just that there is so much to do right now."

'Why right now, Ace?"

"There are things that have their own time to them. Right now it is important that we build this business so you can take your lawyer's advice and sell it at a handsome profit." He sat back and looked at her.

"That is the other thing. You and he talk and

suddenly he is breaking canons of ABA, whatever those are. He waltzes in and tells me the world is going to change. You agree, and both of you tell me to give up my dream." She reached across the table to hold his hands. "What are you two doing? Planning to build the business and then sell it out from under my nose for peanuts?"

"Never."

She leaned back and pulled her hands away. "Are you and the Doctor some kind of bad men on the run, Ace?"

He looked at her for a long moment. "We're not bad men or criminals, though we have learned how to bend the law a bit. You see, there are a lot of people that just go on day by day and never take the time to look around. We have looked, and things are not as those in power would like us to believe. I won't say I haven't hurt people, but they were trying to hurt me or somebody that couldn't fight back. But these are times that require some of us to be resourceful in order to continue our work."

"What is your work, Ace? I know so little about you and yet if you asked me to, I'd walk on your chest in high heels and talk dirty about your mother." She leaned across the table again.

"Sounds good to me." He got up and started to bus some dishes off the tables. "I got about three hours work to do before tomorrow and another herd of hungry townsfolk, so maybe it would be a good idea if you headed upstairs, got a shower, and snuggled up in that big warm bed for some sleep."

"You sound like it's your place," she com-mented, leaning on the jukebox.

"No, just the hired hand."

'We haven't even talked about wages or what you want for all of this." She motioned to the room.

"I want a favor."

"Name it."

"I want you to close next Sunday and go to the cranberry pick at Mallory's." She started to protest but he had raised his hand. "I know. You only close on your birthday and Christmas but this is special. And it is the payment I want."

She stood there and looked at the intensity in his eyes. "Okay."

"Good." He continued to clean tables.

"Ace? The lock on the door upstairs is not locked," she held the door.

"One of these days, Darlin'."

"Are those just words, or can I take that to the bank?" She looked at him with childlike awe. He walked over and gave her a kiss.

"It's already in the bank." He went back to cleaning tables.

He heard the door leading upstairs close quietly and the sound of her steps as she ascended the staircase.

"Well, Ollie, this is another fine mess you've gotten me into, isn't it?" He moved around the room working and humming to himself.

• • • • •

It was five in the morning. Mallory's back had been killing him all night, so he had gotten up and had been working on the computer for awhile. He noticed the light on in the outbuilding. He concluded that either Tesla or Angel had forgotten to turn it off when they finished up for the night. "Well, we don't need some tourist, or worse yet, Deputy Dimwit to come cruising around and find our little friend out there, do we?" He wasn't speaking to anyone, but when he heard the meow he knew he was not alone.

"You still up and home? My God. By now, I thought you would be off killing something harmless and warm-blooded." The cat responded with a low growl. "Only kidding, Haddoxes. Lady Lydia told me that you have sworn to be on your best behavior. Only kidding."

He pulled on an old heavy reefer jacket and a nor'wester that hung by the door and walked toward the building. The first strikes of morning were showing in the east, but the sky was still afire with stars. He opened the door then stopped.

Ace was standing there looking down at the Wasp. It was a work of wonder. The open circular frame was black. The circumference was accented with seven halogen lights covered by different filters. The four-stroke, eighty horsepower motorcycle engine was immaculate. Two counter-rotational propellers were mounted horizontally within the ring. A fiberglass enclosed cockpit with a reflective-coated Plexiglass windscreen was mounted astride the craft. It was eight feet in diameter and four feet high at the highest point. The color was flat black. There were two rings of chrome steel, four inches apart, that ran completely around the bottom of the craft. One of the rings was hooked to the negative lead and one to the positive lead of a high voltage, high frequency discharge coil. In all, it was a work of art.

"Will it fly?" Mallory stood and looked at Ace.

"Oh, it will fly. That's not the problem. How long is the problem." Ace was walking around it and testing different points for rigidity.

"Is it still worth it?" Mallory pulled out his pipe, started to stuff tobacco into it, and then decided to put it back into his pocket.

"She is and what we are doing is." Ace never looked up from the craft. "How long does this *thing* have to be airborne?"

"From the calculations I've made, it will take you seven minutes to cross the Bay and then turn, elevate to a thousand feet, then turn off all the lights and coil and head for the barn."

"The discharge coil?" He pointed to the chrome rings.

"Tesla's idea. They will be discharging about three-quarters of a million volts when you're running."

That should be enough to cause a lot of blurring on film and video cameras. The halogen lights are pointed outward to aid in making it difficult to see the actual outline of the craft, too. The sound of the coil will add to the general confusion of the event. Tesla found an old building about two miles down the road that will be the launch and recovery point."

He walked up next to Ace. "Lindsey hired a couple of Indians to be out there and be ready to pull you out if it augers in on you."

"Lindsey hired?" It was the first time that Ace looked up.

"My thought exactly." Mallory walked over to the table that had been converted to a shop bench. "He knows. I'm not sure how, but I would suspect that our Dark Lady has something to do with it."

"This place is going to be crawling with Feds, you know that, Doc?"

"It is anyway," Mallory looked down at one of the electronic test devices on the bench.

"How come?"

"It looks like the phase shift is going to happen right at the same time. Or two days before." Mallory was watching the oscilloscope pattern and its hypnotic rhythm.

"Is Her Ladyship ready?" "She has her transmitter set up, but the chances of it being one of her ships is one in a hundred."

"I'll hate to see her go, but she is a long way from home." Ace sat down on a stool.

"Aren't we all, my friend? Aren't we all?" With that Mallory walked out of the building without another word.

Ace walked around the craft again, and finally pulled the hatch open and got inside to try the controls. "Talk about messes."

CHAPTER 23

Lindsey needed to see Lydia. He was not sure why, but the feeling was overpowering. It was about ten A.M. when he pulled into the driveway of the old Twitchell place. He parked the Dodge next to her Citroen and walked up the steps to the porch. He strolled into the parlor without knocking or waiting to be announced. She was sitting there at the console of some strange looking device. It resembled a radio, but had very unusual types of knobs and dials. She looked up and caught his eyes surveying both her and the device.

"Caught?" She turned in the chair to face him fully.

"If you make contact are you going to say good-bye to an old friend?" He walked over and sat down in a chair next to her.

"The most important word in that sentence is *if*." She noted the pained look on his face. "Probably the word *friend* is more important, isn't it?"

"I had hoped so." He looked at the machine carefully.

"It has been so long, Clyde. I forget that not everyone understands what it's like to be a visitor in a strange world." She turned back toward him and gently touched his check. "I do care, but it's not good to care too much, for everything is transitory in nature and we will have to part one day — either because of my leaving or your dying."

"Didn't you miss something in all of that? Like, you might die before me?" He walked over and checked the urn to see if there was some coffee. There was, and he motioned to her asking if she wanted a cup. She indicated that she did not. He filled his cup and came back and sat down. He lingered over the smell before starting to drink it.

"No. By your calculations I am much older than you, but we also have a much greater span of life than inhabitants of this·world." She played with the metal charm that hung around her neck.

"How old are you?"

"In your terms, I have just entered middle age." She smiled a gentle smile at her covert statement.

"In standard earth years, Lydia." He sipped his coffee and looked into those blue-within-blue eyes.

"Two hundred and seventy four standard years." Her tone was flat and did not give any hint of threat or worry at giving up the truth.

"Middle age?"

"Entering middle age. I probably have five hundred standard years left in this body before the time of renewal," she again spoke offhandedly.

"Renewal?" He wanted to know so much and felt he would never have the time to learn all he desired.

"A complex theological term which involves the movement of mind from one adaptive being into a fresh body to continue the journey." She closed her eyes.

"A concept of reincarnation or rebirth without losing conscience or memory."

"Fairly accurate. Some refinement in the actual occurrence, but for limited understanding it is quite good." She reached out and touched his hand.

"Limited understanding? A month ago I would have laughed at all of this and thought someone was trying to play a grand joke on me. Now...now I just can't believe all that is happening. I've fallen in love with an alien. I've made friends with two mad men who are most likely on the lists of half a dozen people who think they would be better off dead. I've been talking to a face-shifting cat that is probably something so strange that my mind could not even conceptualize him. And I'm playing a part in a conspiracy that will probably get us all killed, jailed, or deported to some remote asteroid in a distant solar system." He sat back in total exasperation.

"Nobody has sent anyone into exile on an asteroid in at least a thousand years." She smiled again.

"See? It's not strange to you, but from my point of view, the whole thing is like I dropped right into a Rod Serling teleplay. 'Now, folks, with your approval let me introduce you to our players!' Sure, it's easy for you. You understand all of this and live with it. Me? I'm just a guy who wanted to get away from the world and forget about all of the crap I ever had to deal with. The dirty deals, fat businessmen, dumb starlets, corrupt politicians, and other lawyers that made sharks look like acceptable company. So, I move to East Jesus Nowhere and start out in a new life, letting myself put all my emotions on the shelf and not ever having to worry about any of this junk again. And what happens? You walk into my office and I'm in the middle of something that no one, and I repeat, no one, would ever believe." He had been pacing around the room looking more like Mallory than himself.

"Calm yourself, Clyde. It is not the end of the world." She got up and walked over to him.

"Does this mean nothing to you? Everything that I have said, nothing at all?" He ran his hand through his hair and looked completely perplexed.

"Of course it does. But you want me to tell you that I love you and care and that we can always be together? That would not be the truth. I am not one of you. I am different and I desire things also. I have people I care about and wish to see again, and I long for the purple hills of my home and the two suns that give warmth. It is not like I don't care about you...I would not have shared my Ortilium with you if you meant nothing." She held him gently in her arms.

"Ortilium?"

"My essence. We shared something that you may come to find to be a curse. By your time frame, I have given you an extension to your life. You will neither age nor die for many years. You will outlive friends and family. I hope you never come to curse my memory for that." He saw her eyes tear up and a single tear fall slowly down her cheek. "I have given you the water of my life."

"How long?"

"Does it matter?"

"Only because I have curiosity."

"You will live, barring an accident, for one hundred and twenty standard years. You will remain in your present form, aging little, and not losing thought or memory. Is that such a bad gift between friends?"

"No." His tone was flat.

"You desire more and longer. But the truth is, there is no more to give. You have the best there is, and, as far as *longer* goes, there would be difficulties. I cannot give up trying to go home. I have responsibilities and family. I must continue to try. It is our way. And if not now, then sometime one of my people will come through and I will go. I must." She looked truly hurt for the first time. "I have no choice."

"How did you come to be here?" He sat back down holding her hand.

"It is a long story. I am an Ortlus, a diplomat of sorts. I was carrying a message between my world and an outlying planet in another system. We were two parsec out of my home world of Stygian in what you call the Zeta Reticulum System — a quasi binary. It actually has five suns in the system. We were in hypersleep when Haddoxes awakened me to the reality that we had punched through a hole in the space-time continuum and were in your world's gravity field. There was no hope of escaping, because when we passed through, our navigation system was destroyed by the energy pulse and we crashed."

She wrapped her hands around her shoulders as if trying to warm herself. Turning with tears in her eyes, she looked at him.

Clyde said, "I have thought only of my own desire and my own pain. I did not think of yours. For that, I am truly sorry. I am not sorry for caring for or loving you. But as you point out so well, we are simple creatures, not realizing that other sentient beings in the universe have feelings as well." He turned to go. Mallory stood in the doorway, a cold pipe in his mouth. He was looking at Lady Lydia. The spoken truth hung heavy in the room.

"Counselor." Mallory stood to one side of the doorway.

"Dr. Mallory. Whatever I can do to assist you over the next few days, you have but to ask." Lindsey stood there, not sure of what tack to take in his course. His head was swimming with thoughts and emotions.

"It is going to become very crazy very quickly around here. I need you to offer the sound voice of reason and make sure nobody gets too close to her

Ladyship or Haddoxes. The rest we will take care of, Clyde." Mallory handed Lindsey a detailed schedule of what he foresaw as the plan of action.

"It would be my pleasure." He turned and looked back at Lydia who was still standing by the window. "I would be honored if you two would have dinner with me tonight at Dixie Raye's."

"That would be nice." Lydia smiled and Mallory nodded.

Lindsey walked out into the filtered sunlight and over to the Dodge station wagon. He fished for the keys in his pocket and came up with them and a piece of gum. He unwrapped the gum and popped it into his mouth then slid behind the wheel. He sat there for a minute before starting the car and heading back to Clover Bay and his reality.

WAYNE E. HALEY

CHAPTER 24

The Colonel was sitting at the Panic Desk of T & C at Hemispherical Defense Command Headquarters in Cheyenne, Wyoming when the alarm went off. The pulsing red light on the console was strobing for no more than two seconds when the Colonel picked up the red phone on the right-hand side of the desk. He hit the single black button on the instrument and waited until he heard the tone go off.

"This is Skyhook. We have a Firestorm Condition One. Repeat, this is Skyhook. We have a Firestorm Condition One. Code two Bravo Alpha. Repeat, two Bravo Alpha. Sector five, grid coordinates three Henry Victor, seven November. Send a Team. Priority One. Repeat, Priority One."

He replaced the phone, unlocked the drawer on the right, and pulled out the manual. He initialed the entry then returned the book to the desk and locked the drawer. His task was done, and yet he did not know what a Firestorm was. He had only followed the orders required for these occasions. He had told his wife that often he thought this was nothing more than a test run of some kind to see what type of response alertness HDC had. He knew this did not have anything to do with a nuclear alert or pending invasion. So it seemed to him that this had to be a test alert of some kind. Especially since they occurred so infrequently and at such random places.

He went back to his copy of Popular Science and continued to study the plans for a small bookcase made of wood. He was planning to build it on the following weekend.

· · · · ·

It took less than fifteen minutes for the mobile response team stationed at Fallon, Nevada to be airborne. They were in full traveling gear, and each man carried two fiberglass cases as they climbed into the small jet that was constantly ready on the ramp.

Seven men loaded themselves and their gear into the airplane, and the chief security officer handed the pilot a chart with indicator points marked on it.

The team was thrust into the sky with the knowledge that they would be on the ground probably twenty-six hours before the first pulse of the gateway would show up. The instruments aboard the KH-11 satellite that had detected the first ripple in the space-time fabric had immediately flashed the warning and the second pulse had confirmed that an occurrence was getting ready to happen. It could be any time within a span of twenty-six to seventy hours before the breach would be opened. The security team from Firestorm knew that they had to be on the ground and ready. Logistics at Wright Paterson AFB was already gearing up for another arrival. One in four Firestorms seemed to have an "occurrence" that produced researchable evidence.

The tightest run security system in the world and the best kept secret the world has ever known was about to be tested again. And all of those involved knew that this was another chance the whole house of cards might come tumbling down around their ears.

The Shrub was out of position and nobody was going to tell the Duck anything. So when the Firestorm phone rang in the situation room in the basement of the rented house in Washington D.C., the presidential Chief of Staff listened carefully. He made no notes and walked to the safe that contained the detailed instructions, a format that was initiated during the Harry Truman administration. He pulled the special yellow folder out and ran his finger down the list of those people that had a "need to know." His first call would be to Camp David. It was his duty to let the boss know that the country, if not the world, was hours away from yet another Armageddon. His next call would be to the bubble chamber where all war planning was done.

If the boss said, "Do it," he would relay the call

through the special security phone system and have the old man tell the Joint Chiefs to put everyone on alert and start the cover story that the Chinese were milling about, or that some third-world jerk was playing nuclear blackmail again. He put the file down, picked up the phone, and rang up Camp David. The phone rang three times before the voice answered.

"Tell the boss we've got a Firestorm over Washington State and Two Bravo Alpha is airborne out of NAS Fallon. ETA five-zero minutes. I will be here waiting his reply."

He hung up the phone and took his glasses off. He was a devoted Christian and a person who, even though he had attained the high position of Chief of Staff, still had what he considered morals and ethics. This did not make sense to him. Yet he had seen the proof. It still struck him as unreal and not within his religious reality, yet he knew it to be true. If the experts were right, one of these Firestorms would bring with it a day like no other anyone has ever expected, and it would make December seventh look like a picnic. He put his head down on the table in the same place both LBJ and Nixon had put their heads, in hopes that this, too, would pass. Just another flap with no major problems. Just some scared civilians who would need to be silenced. He waited for the next call.

CHAPTER 25

Nobody in Clover Bay could remember a cranberry picking that started at three in the afternoon. But this strange doctor out on the north side of the Bay had his own way of doing things, and if it took putting up with a late afternoon pick to get the berries and have a nearly free meal, well, that was okay. The folks of Clover Bay knew what a good thing a free meal could be, especially since that new cook at Dixie Raye's diner was going to be whipping up some ribs and salmon on the grill. Most folks had been talking about the fact that even Dixie Raye was closing up for the occasion. This was something really special. And if her place was closed, then it meant they would have to either eat at home or take some dip and chips and go out to Mallory's and have some ribs and salmon and somebody else's chips and dip.

Clyde had told people that the Doctor would not have the pick in the morning because he did not want to interfere with worship services at the local churches. This pleased the two parsons, and both agreed that it would be a good idea to promote understanding this day and recommended that everyone go out and meet the new folks at the old Twitchell place on Bay Road.

Mallory had calculated that the local sundown was at 5:10 P.M. So it would give people about an hour-and-a-half to pick their fill of cranberries and load them up in the cars. Then they'd get the victuals out and put them on the tables he'd supplied and placed conveniently along the south side of the porch. The ribs and salmon would be served right at 5:32 P.M. He had also calculated that at 5:41 there would be enough people on the lawn and porch to see the light show over the Bay, and they'd still have a margin of error of four minutes.

Ace and Mallory had spent four hours cooking and prepping everything so there would be nothing to do the last minute except serve up the main course. Lady Lydia had moved the transceiver upstairs and Haddoxes would be watching it to see if any signals were coming in through the gateway. Angel was down at the old barn with the craft doing final preparations. She had told Mallory that she did not want to be a pagan feeding with a bunch of Protestants, anyway.

Everyone was a little on edge except Tesla. He was lying in the parlor face down on the carpet, dead exhausted from three days and nights of unending work. He was listening to the broadsides that Angel kept up all the time they were working. The last thing he had said, or rather signed to Mallory, was that he had truly considered returning to his ancestral habit of killing barbarians, especially those dressed in ecclesiastical robes — male or female, it did not matter which.

Mallory had noted that he had never seen anyone sleep with their face straight down and arms to their sides. Holding his platter of salmon, Ace passed the living room and stopped. He looked at Tesla, shook his head, and walked out to the porch. As Mallory turned to help him, Ace said, "That boy is not asleep. He's in one of those damn hypnotic trances that you taught him. He is only breathing about once a minute right now."

"It's okay. He earned the rest. Putting up with a woman like Angel would make most men want to get an Alabama divorce." Mallory was tasting the salmon.

"What the hell is an 'Alabama divorce'?"

"That is where you shoot your wife to put her out of YOUR misery." Mallory walked down the stairs and, watching the cars start to arrive, began pointing them toward various parking areas.

"Oh, boy." Ace walked back inside and shuffled back into the kitchen where Dixie Raye was making sauce to go with the ribs. "Well, they're starting to show up, bags in hand and grins on their faces!" He slapped her on the backside as he walked around the cutting table.

"Only do that if you mean it, Cowboy," she

winked at him.

"You bet, lady. And then some." He leaned up against the sink and looked right at her.

"We'll see won't we?"

"You can bet your sweet...," he was interrupted by Tesla wandering in and heading toward the fridge for something to eat. "Tesla, there is a ton of food in there. What would you like?"

Tesla opened the fridge looked around at the ribs and salmon and various pastries. He pulled out a bowl of cold rice and took a pair of chopsticks from his pocket. He sat down in the corner of the room and started to eat. His bloodshot eyes looked highly magnified through his Coke-bottle lenses. He shoveled what seemed like three mouthfuls of rice into his open maw and chomped down. He signed to Ace and went back to his eating.

"What did he say?" Dixie Raye looked over at Ace who was laughing to himself.

"He thinks you've got a cute ass."

"Is that really what he said?" She put a hand on her waist and turned to look at a smiling Tesla.

"Something like that. It loses a little bit in translation, but the meaning is about the same."

"He isn't so dumb after all, is he?" she cringed at her own words.

"Well, that's a hell of a way to win friends my dear." Ace signed back at Tesla.

"Wait a minute. He can hear. Why do you two always make sign language to him? That is for those that are hearing impaired." She turned, looking a little exasperated.

"We sign in Japanese. It's the only way to communicate complex ideas."

Ace was still signing when Dixie Raye interrupted again. "Now that just doesn't make sense to me at all."

"Good." Ace picked up a platter and walked out of the kitchen leaving Dixie looking down at Tesla and him looking up at her and grinning between bites.

"What have you got yourself into, girl? This just doesn't happen in Sand Creek, now does it?" She went back to mixing up some more sauce and laughing to herself.

· · · · ·

Folks had been picking cranberries for about an hour-and-a-half. The old fields had yielded a good crop and everyone seemed happy. Pastor Dan Brown was standing on the porch making small talk with Doc when Clyde approached. "How are you, Pastor?"

"Fine Mr. Lindsey. We haven't seen you at services in the last few weeks. We have missed you." Pastor Dan was doing his best genial-guilt act.

"Oh, I have been really busy trying to make sure that the ferry service is not lost. Would you excuse the Doctor and me a moment? I need his advice on something." Lindsey moved Doc out of hearing range with a smile.

"Just tell them, Clyde, what we're planning, why don't ye?" Mallory filled his pipe.

"Easy Doc, I was just talking to Deputy Dimwit and he tells me that some government types showed up this morning, took over his substation, and had a bunch of radios and other communications equipment. Has it started?"

"Sounds that way. Oh, boy, The Cult of Silence. 'Into the breach again we go'...," Mallory walked away without another word. He put his happy face back on, handshaking and slapping backs like he was running for president or dogcatcher of the county.

CHAPTER 26

By late afternoon, the crowd was milling about the deck overlooking the Bay. The sun hit the horizon with an inaudible thud, and the first stars were beginning to shine over Useless Bay. Some folks had already departed with their gunnysacks of cranberries. These people did not want to stay around to see any more of this strange group now that they had their yearly supply of cranberries. Within days, the berries would be put up into preserves and jellies in anticipation of Thanksgiving and Christmas.

For those that remained, the evening was turning out to be fun. Doc was moving about the crowd, telling stories and meeting a lot of folks. Clyde was doing the same, making small talk, much of which was about the upcoming meeting concerning the ferry service to Clover Bay. Ace had been putting food out and making sure everybody had something to eat and drink. Deputy Bob was walking around the grounds and doing his basic snooping. Well before the event, however, the whole place had been sanitized. Lady Lydia and Haddoxes had locked themselves in the old blue room on the top floor of the Twitchell house to stay out of sight and maintain their watch on the computers and transceiver. Dixie Raye was still working in the kitchen, more out of choice than need. Making small talk with the folks she served everyday was not high on her hit parade. In order not to attract attention when it left, Tesla had parked one of the vehicles just up the lane from the house.

At ten minutes past five, Mallory walked over to Ace, pointed to the flagpole and mumbled something. Ace descended the steps to the lawn and pulled the three-colored pink flag down and folded it up. He walked back into the house and turned the stereo on. The music was soft and relaxing and filtered unobtrusively out onto the deck where folks were having a good time eating and chatting.

Ace had walked into the kitchen and whispered to Dixie Raye that he needed to go into town and pick up Angel. He had mentioned that she was visiting one of the local Catholics, but needed to get back to the house before it got too late.

"Do you want me to come along with you?"

"No, that's okay. I'll only be gone half-an-hour or so, and Doc gets really nervous if somebody isn't here that knows something about making food." He winked at her.

"You just want to be alone with another woman,

don't you?" Dixie Raye leaned back and stared at him, not revealing any of her true feelings.

"You bet," he smiled and turned, "see you in a few, Darlin'."

With that, and before she could respond, he was out the backdoor and jogging down the path to the roadway. He checked his chronograph and pushed the start button on his stopwatch.

The car was exactly where he expected to find it. The engine had already been started, and he knew Tesla would be on his way back to the house. Ace accelerated down the lane and checked his rear view mirror repeatedly to see if anyone was following. He had driven this route four times in the last two days to check the time and speed required to get from the house to the old shed they had picked for their purpose. He swung through the open doors of the large building. Angel immediately closed them behind him. It was totally dark in the shed with the doors closed, so Ace flipped on the headlights. In their glow sat the Wasp, black and ready to fly. They had wound it up a couple of times, but had not yet taken it off the ground for fear of being seen. This, then, would be the maiden voyage and possibly the last if Ace was not really careful.

As he was zipping up his black jumpsuit, Angel hung a St. Michael's medal around Aces's neck. "This is the patron saint of sinners, drunks, and flyers — all of which pertain to you, Liebchen."

"Gee, thanks." Ace was, as usual, underwhelmed by the thought of depending upon any nickel-and-dime ornament to keep his life from flashing in front of his eyes in half a second, in black and white and not very interesting.

"She'll yaw to the left on takeoff, so stand on that right rudder pedal. But back it off quick when you're in flight, otherwise you're going to be swimming." She opened the cockpit and gave him a hand getting in.

Ace buckled up and quickly eyeballed all the flight controls. "Well, for all our sins may we truly be forgiven. Clear!"

Before she could reply, he had hit the magneto-starter and eighty horses jumped to life in a deafening roar. She snapped off the headlights on the Dodge station wagon and pushed the Bay side door open. The last hint of yellow-orange hung on the western horizon just above the fog bank.

Ace knew the trick in flying a Wasp was in the balance control. For directional flight it was required that you lean in the direction of desired travel and then compensate with a fan adapter built into the toroidal housing between the two props. With a neutral balance attitude, the craft would only ascend and descend, depending on the amount of throttle given. In theory it seemed really simple. In reality it had all the fun of getting kicked in the ribs by a mule.

• • • • •

Mallory stood and looked at his watch. It was

show time. He noticed the location of each of his future witnesses. Pastor Dan stood next to Mildred and Harv. They were sharing small talk and some of the smoked salmon. Knots of people hung around the porch and some had descended to the lawn area to stand and chat while they ate their fill.

Mallory watched as Dixie Raye came out with another platter of desert that looked creamy and white. He looked at her and realized that a very big part of this was about her. No, that was not really true. He had pretended, even to himself, that this was the case, but in reality it was about events and other people's desires to silence the truth. She was just the crux of it, his own personal focus — the cause that would unite them into action more than just studying the phenomena. He understood more the difference between himself and Ace. Ace was a man of pure action where Mallory had been a man of thought. Ace had focused the problem in human terms and exploded a random event into a force of good for her and these people. Somehow it was all tied together. Simple people's lives. Like the bean counters at the ferry, the mystery men from the government trying to hide the truth, and Lady Lydia who just wanted to go home. She was not here by her desire. It struck him funny that a diner owner in Washington and a Royal Heir to a throne twenty light-years away could share the same desire. They just wanted to live their lives and find some degree of happiness without being interfered with by outside forces.

Tesla had resumed from preparing the station wagon. Mallory noticed him as he walked out the backdoor carrying a huge lensed camera and tripod. They knew that they must have the very best photographs they could get. He stared at his watch again and fumbled for his lighter in the pocket of his tweed jacket.

It was show time.

CHAPTER 27

There was a bank of cellular phones set up in the office of Deputy Bob. Inside, the two watch officers were checking the portable gear and the one outside was hooking up a remote satellite array to give the Firestorm Team a clear channel to the Situation Room and to the Control Center at Fallon NAS.

One man pushed in the coded flash-message buttons and let the computer system lock into the main frame fifteen hundred miles away. They were set to go. Flash traffic could be routed both ways now, bi-directional. Each part of the team was now connected to the others by this invisible umbilical cord.

The shifts would be divided into two watches of twelve hours on and twelve off. They had picked up a large R.V. at the NAS where they had landed on Wibley Island, and had it set up outside the office. They would use it for sleeping, eating, and recreation for the next three days. If an event did occur, it would also serve as the on-site Situation Room to house those that would be coming from D.C. and other stations.

Most of these men had previously been on deployment with Firestorm. They knew the routine by heart. If an incident occurred, they were to shut down the area for communications and traffic, both in and out, until a Blue Team showed up to suppress the locals from talking. "National security" would be the cover, and everyone would be required to sign agreements or suffer the consequences. This was a problem in heavily populated areas, but a place like Clover Bay would be a piece of cake. The shift officer seated himself in the chair behind the desk and started flipping through a copy of *National Rifleman*.

• • • • •

It was a little jumpy coming out of the barn, but Ace was using all the skill to handle the Wasp that his twelve thousand hours of flying had given him. He was at two hundred feet before he could make out the Twitchell Place on his starboard side. He hit the throttle for everything it had, adjusted his position for quick movement, and then placed his hands on the generator and light-control box. He was humming an old 'Sons of the Pioneers' tune, then said under his breath, "And now folks, coming out of chute number five on a Powder River bronc...let her rip, cowboy... spur her at every creek crossing and wash...Yahoo!"

With that, he snapped on the high voltage generator and watched the edge light up in an electric blue corona of sparks. He pressed the switches for the halogen lights and the night was alive like the inside of a disco. He dropped the tape that Tesla had made of high voltage discharge sounds amplified a hundred times into the tape player and cranked the volume control up to the ten peg on the small stereo tape player between his legs. The two Bose subwoffers exploded the tranquility of the night. He aimed at the flagpole on the lawn and then made a hard turn over the Bay, coming short of the beach by five hundred feet.

Pastor Dan was the first to see the electrical discharge over the tree line. Then, when the lights came on, most of the people on the lawn turned to see what was happening. When the air ripped open with the sound of the chariots of fire over the Bay, there was nothing but panic on the lawn and porch. Some folks fell to the ground and started to cry or scream or cover their faces. Some knew that the end of the world had just cleared the tree line. Harv watched very carefully. He had seen a similar sight when he was seventeen in Dutch Harbor, Alaska. The Nips had come in out of the dark and bombed the living hell out of his outfit. He had automatically pulled up his old Nikon that still had eight exposures left. Pastor Dan was shooting pictures with his small fully automatic 35mm that the townsfolk had paid for with donations in the Sunday collection plate at a quarter and buck apiece.

Deputy Bob had pulled his Smith and Wesson 357 Magnum from its holster, and was trying to find his sight pattern. Mallory was standing on the porch and saw the Deputy's weapon. Mallory made sure no one was watching him. He picked up a half-full bowl of punch and ran toward the spot where Deputy Bob was standing about ten feet below him. Mallory looked up at the craft going by and yelled out some incomprehensible monosyllabic nothing and dropped the bowl directly down on Deputy Dimwit's head. The man dropped like a steer in the slaughterhouse pelted with a sledgehammer between the eyes. Deputy and gun went sprawling onto the lawn.

Lothak and Michael were in the boat directly below the Wasp when it made its run at the house. Lothak looked up from his beer and handed it to his son. "Flies okay for a Robertson Wasp, doesn't it?"

Michael was pulling a 45-pound salmon into the boat. He looked up and then back to the fish. "Needs some better directional stabilization. If he banks it too hard, it's going to bust the main rotor shaft." He hit the fish on its head with a short club.

"Should have used one of those German engines. Would have been better." Lothak pulled the starter on the Evenrude outboard. "Looks like we can head for home and catch the kickoff of the Dolphins at Dallas."

"Good. Too damn cold to fish any way." Michael put the fish into a bag. He turned to watch the craft go out of sight over the far tree line on the other side of the Bay. "Think he will make it in?"

"This time. But he better watch those turns coming out of the climb." Both bundled up and skimmed over the water toward the path which they had figured Ace would use to return to the barn.

"Did you see that, Pastor? What was it?" Mallory was clinging to Pastor Dan's arm.

"Well, it seemed like...no, it couldn't have been. There are no other living creatures beside...but it...no...well...we have pictures to look at...but...."

"It was a flying saucer wasn't it?" Dixie Raye was standing by Pastor Dan and Mallory.

"It looked like one, but...." Mallory turned to get confirmation from the minister.

"Yes it was, but...," Pastor Dan was quickly losing ground on the fundamental beliefs.

"It was an honest-to-God UFO, right here in Clover Bay." Clyde Lindsey had joined the group that was standing on the porch.

"Yes it was, and we need to call the authorities." Belief system or not, Pastor Dan knew a good thing when it dropped in his hands. He could already see the headlines on the cover of the *Episcopal Times* or maybe the *National Enquirer*. "Minister photographs alien craft while comforting his flock."

"May I use your phone, Dr. Mallory?" Pastor Dan could see the check now in his hands and the new Saturn in his driveway.

"Of course, it's in the parlor." Mallory showed him the way.

A minute later, Ace and Angel pulled into the driveway. Jumping from the car, they ran to the porch. "Did you folks see that 'thing' out over the water?" Ace asked.

Several mumbled answers sprang from various corners of the porch and yard. Angel was leaning over Deputy Bob who was returning to the land-of-the-living after being the first victim of an alien attack to his knowledge. She helped him to his feet, recovered his gun, and pushed it back into his holster.

"Must be shock." She turned to no one in general, but spoke to the ambient air around her.

"Shock, hell! Sorry, Sister. It was something from that ship! It fired on me!" Like handling a rag doll, she helped him to the steps and eased him down gently.

"You saw it while driving up the road?" Dixie Raye was next to Ace.

"Sure did. I have always wanted to see one and now I have." He pulled a Camel from his pocket and noticed his hands were shaking.

"Scared you?" she looked up into his eyes.

"Thought I was going to die at one point," he thought very quickly, "from fright."

CHAPTER 28

Phillip Lewis Stewart was manning the flash communicator at the Firestorm alert position in Clover Bay, Washington. He had been with Firestorm for six years. He had transferred in as a GS-13, and had advanced in those six years to a GS-17. He loved his work and the importance it gave him to think that he was protecting the U.S., if not the world, from the most dangerous event that has ever happened in world history. Phil Stewart knew that Firestorm was the lending edge of attack on the unknown. At his job, he was one of the finest. He didn't have to think very hard. Everything was prepared in the huge red manual that gave him instructions for every possible contingency. If all else failed, he could always pick up the flash communicator telephone handset and speak with someone at Fallon, or Montalk, or the Bubble, and ask for a second opinion — especially if he did not have a first one or a clue as to where to find one.

It was approximately zero two hundred hours Zulu when the red light on the communicator lit up indicating that flash traffic was coming in off the bird. The signal originated in D.C., traveled twenty-six thousand miles out to a geostationary satellite and then back down another twenty-six thousand miles. All of it was in an encrypted format with only the header not encrypted, so it would activate the remote communication station and notify the duty officer that there was an important message or flash traffic coming in. Stewart picked up the handset and spoke his normal reply to this type of situation.

"This is Clover Bay. Stewart, Duty Officer."

"What in the hell is going on out there? You guys are on deck and nobody's calling in spotting reports except civilians, and they are tying up the goddamn phone circuits between Portland and Vancouver. What are you sons-a-bitches doing out there, playing with yourselves?" The voice was too clear on the flash communicator not to know who it was.

"There is no distortion on any of the meters, Sir." Stewart was rechecking all the equipment. Everything seemed to be working just fine.

"I don't give a good goddamn about meters, man. I'm getting all kinds of calls from aides that are telling me that there are a half-a-dozen reports already, and that an occurrence has happened and a boomer came through!" Stewart could just imagine the face that went with the voice at the other end of the phone.

He would be in his blue warmup jacket over a white shirt and tie. Right about now, he would be sitting in the room ready to strangle the living shit out of anybody that walked in.

"Where...Sir? Do you have any idea where it happened?" Stewart felt that he was losing ground quickly.

"Now, isn't that just special? What do we pay you, maybe fifty thousand a year? We fly your ass around the country on taxpayers' dollars, give you fun toys to play with, and the power to just about rape and plunder half the world with our consent. And you ask me where it happened!" The voice trailed off for a moment and Stewart heard an exchange of gruff voices in the background. The voice returned to the dedicated carrier. "Now listen, you moron. The occurrence happened someplace within a few miles of you. That is why you are there — to find out about it, discredit it, or shut the whole goddamn place down or blow it off the face of the map. I don't give a shit what you do, but you had better start doing something really fast. Elsewise, I am personally going to get on my big white bird, fly out there and blow your goddamn head off."

By the end of the monologue, Stewart was holding the handset a good ten inches from his ear and still suffered from the sound level coming down the line.

"Yes...Yes Sir, right away, Sir...." The line went dead.

Stewart reached over and hit the remote wireless

intercom that hooked up the duty station in the Deputy's office with the R.V. He hit it three times. "We got one! A Firestorm! And the boss is raging! Drop your cocks and grab your socks. Let's move!"

Within minutes the four other duty officers and two security officers were assembled in the room. They were exchanging glances and looking at the monitoring equipment. Nothing was showing. One of the men looked at Stewart. "Who called? You said 'the boss.' Dr. Hargrove from Fallon?"

"Negative. The Boss from the Camp."

"How in the hell would he know about this if nobody in the link knows?"

Stewart thought for a moment. It was a good question. "Doesn't matter, he does, so we go to phase one. HUMINT. Human Intelligences. Brake up into sectors and see what's going on around here. Report back every thirty minutes via radio. Now, move it!" Stewart had already pulled out the blue book and started a timing and sighting series observation report.

Each man started out in different directions. They had to know what was happening, and quickly, if the boss already knew. This whole operation depended on speed. If there was an occurrence, and a boomer came through, then they had to close it down quickly. That was the whole mission of Firestorm. Right now it did not appear that they were doing it very well.

. . . . .

Tesla had just walked into the living room. All of the guests had left about thirty minutes before, and the main electric gate had been closed and secured again. Tesla held the wet prints of the first printed series of photographs. He had blown them up to glossy eight-by-tens and handed them to Mallory, who was studying the computer printout. Mallory looked slowly through each one and then went through them again. Each one showed enough light patterns and an electrical discharge field to obscure the view of the craft. He looked up and smiled his wily grin. "Dry them and get ready to drive to Seattle tonight. You can get there by midnight, and these will be in the morning papers. Lady Lydia has already called an old friend and he is waiting for them."

Tesla signed very quickly.

"I know...," he turned back to the monitor on the right. "It's a 'flash traffic' coming in on the EGS-13 bird and downlink. The computer only could decrypt some of it. But they are aware, so things are going to heat up around here."

Tesla moved to the basement door without any other comment. He descended to dry the prints and get them ready for delivery.

Lady Lydia walked into the room just as Tesla was leaving and nodded to him. She walked over to Mallory's side and watched the monitors.

"They will know very soon that it is not a distortion. Then what will they do?"

Mallory sat and looked outside into the dark night. "They will try first to determine if it is a hoax. Then, when they find there are so many witnesses, they will go up to phase two and start to scram this place and shut the information flow off until they calculate if a micro opening occurred. It will take time, maybe a day or two. But then they will seal this place up like the plague descended on it."

"Do you think we have time for one more run?" She sat down next to him.

"I don't know. We are approaching the gateway time and I sure don't want to screw up the possibility of you finding a legation ship, if you can." He pulled off the printout and handed it to her. "It will be one of the bigger flaps. The gate will be open for anywhere from an hour to six hours standard time. In the wormhole of space, that could mean ten or twelve standard days."

"That would give enough time for a signal and a reply via transdermal communicator." She sat back and stared at the old ornate ceiling in the room. "Oh, Doc, if this is the time for it, what have we done?"

"It was a calculated risk." He sat back and closed his eyes and made some mental notes. "This is longer than anyone could have predicted up to this point. The electromagnetic buildup just went over the red line about an hour ago. Those clowns at Fallon will know within the hour as well, I would hope, but maybe we are just that much ahead of them. Getting you and Haddoxes out of here, if you can make contact and set a meeting, will be a trick without these guys getting in our way."

"Home. It almost frightens me." She sat forward and reached out to hold Mallory's hand. "I can't even dream of what has happened."

"Will you remember your friends when you're back on your home world?" The voice came from the entry hall and it came from the rumpled man standing in the doorway. Clyde Lindsey was standing there looking at both of them. His voice was not filled with care, hope, or sarcasm. It was only a question.

"Of course. How could I not?" She walked over and put her arm around his waist and led him back into the room.

"Oh, it seems like in comparison to you, and from what I can understand of your world, we must be as primitive as bushmen to you." Clyde walked over toward the computers.

"Speak for yourself, counselor. Some of us feel superior to any race we've met." Mallory was stuffing his pipe.

"You would," the cynicism filled the room.

"Of course. And so should you. But...." Mallory threw his hands up in a gesture of exasperation.

"Well, it would look like we are going to be the talk of the Pacific Northwest. I just got off the phone with a half dozen different newspapers that were calling me, because I was the only lawyer that was listed. I bet they were calling anybody that had a phone. We also have some unfriendlies talking to people, trying to get a clear picture of what happened. They are not turning down the screws, yet, but they don't appear to be happy with what they are hearing from folks. The one that they can't shut up is Dimwit. He is down at Dixie's telling everyone that he was shot by a spaceman with a ray gun!" Lindsey sat opposite both of them and played with a piece of string on the arm of the chair.

"Nobody has used ray guns in half a dectar. Not at least in my quarter of the galaxy." She looked actually astonished at the thought.

"Demon for details. That is what I like in a cop. Clear insight and ability to put a puzzle together. Tax money well spent." Mallory got up and walked toward the door. "I am hungry. Want anything?"

"No."

"No thank you, Doc. But if you see Haddoxes tell him that I would like to see him." Lady Lydia moved next to Lindsey in the old chair that was Margaret Twitchell's favorite — the one covered in a faded rose pattern popular in the 1930s.

"Worthless piece of space scum. Sure, if I see him I shall send him to Your Ladyship." With that, Mallory lumbered down the hall toward the rear of the house and the repository of copious amounts of leftovers.

Lindsey turned to her and looked into those blue-within-blue eyes. "It would appear that you are going to have the chance to get off this coil?"

"Possibly, but nothing is certain. We have tried three times before, but the gateway has not been open as long as it will be this time. This could be a good chance." She noted the pain in the man's eyes as he watched her speak.

"I shall miss you. I know that you might not make contact. But I also know that if you do, we may not have a chance to say good-bye properly. So I thought it would be best to do it now." He stood up and started to walk toward the doorway.

"It would be better if we did it in the morning, wouldn't it?" She got up and walked next to him.

"Huh...?"

"Is the Temporal Discontinuity returning?" She took his hand in hers.

"Must be; I just went blank."

She walked toward the staircase still holding his hand. He followed like a trusting child. "I am not sure...ah."

"You don't have to be. I am." She walked with him up the staircase that led to Margaret Twitchell's old bedroom, which overlooked the north side of Useless Bay.

WAYNE E. HALEY

CHAPTER 29

The last of the townsfolk had left Dixie Raye's place and the front door was locked. The neon sign that hung outside was turned off and the street seemed deserted. It was about 11:30 P.M. in Clover Bay.

She had returned and opened the bar section just because so many people wanted a place to go and talk. It had been one of the best nights in the bar that she could remember. Everyone had been talking and debating about what exactly it was they had seen out at the old Twitchell place. The shock of the moment had passed, and each person was trying to make the observable facts fit into their own personal cosmology of the universe.

Dixie had agreed with everyone and kept pouring shots and pulling beers. Ace sat at the end of the bar, quieter than Dixie Raye had ever seen him in the two months that she had known him. He smoked and drank, listening to various descriptions of the flight. He had added little to the conversation with the exception of underscoring the fact that what had been seen had to be extraterrestrial, and that it had picked this little bit of nowhere for its show.

As she finished dumping the water in the basin of the back bar, she walked up next to him and wiped her hands on the bar towel. She moved onto the stool next to him and wiped down a nonexistent spot on the bar. "Seems to me like that 'thing' had more of an effect on you than anybody else, Cowboy."

"Why would you say that, Darlin'?" He faced her full on.

"Because it seems to me that you would lead the lynch mob normally. Yet, you just listened a lot tonight." She continued to rub the spot with the dish towel.

"Me? No, just a student of things. And this needs some study." He got up and made his way to the coffee pot and filled his cup. "'Sides, everyone out there saw what they saw. Don't do any good trying to convince them otherwise. There will be plenty of folks trying to do that soon enough."

"What do you mean by that?" She sat a little straighter on the stool.

"Did you see those two old boys in the corner tonight?"

"Yeah. The ones in the cheap suits? So?" She looked in the direction of the booth where they had been sitting, as if they were still there or that their afterimage might have remained.

"Feds. Seen that type before. Right now they are asking simple questions, but in a day or two they will be telling people what everybody saw. And it will be a light-refracting effect caused by random movements of northern lights or some super secret government project, and everyone will be told to keep their mouths shut, or else." He returned to the stool and sipped at his coffee.

"Or else what?" She didn't like the tone of the conversation at all and wanted to know why he suddenly knew so much about it.

"Seen it before. Elko, Nevada...; Great Falls, Montana..., Gulf Port, Texas. A couple of places in Kansas and once up on the Vermont/New York border. They don't want people talking about this kind of thing, and they will do a lot to make sure that they don't."

"You're frightening me, Ace." She put her arm through his. "You make it sound like they would do anything to make folks believe they didn't see anything tonight. But we did."

"Sure we did. And so have a lot of others, but that's not the point. They want to keep this whole thing under raps. Tomorrow you will have twenty more guys like that nosing around town. Then some Air Force 'brass' will show up with impressive credentials, and they will sound reassuring and some folks will listen. Then little by little, it will fade away." He looked at her and laughed. "Listen to me...." He got up and reached for his old leather flight jacket.

"It's a cold night out there, Cowboy."

He walked to the door and stood for a minute looking out at the clear sky and the stars that were dancing heel and toe with each other. "You're right."

He reached up and shut the inside lights off. This only left the juke box and the small beer sign behind the bar to illuminate the room. He walked back to her and she watched him carefully as he put his coat down in the booth next to the juke box.

"Rain check time, Cowboy?" She moved off the stool and undid her hair and shook it free.

"Nope."

She looked at him with a puzzled expression.

"Not a rain check. I just want to be with one person tonight. 'Cause right now," he had put his arms around her waist, "all that I hold dear I am holding."

"Good line." The sarcasm was heavy in her voice.

"If it was a line, I would agree."

She looked into those blue eyes and realized that there was nothing but honesty being offered. She reached over and pulled the chain on the beer sign, walked to the door that led upstairs and opened it. She stood there a minute and then reached out a hand to take his. "Come on up here, Cowboy. You can give me the backrub I need."

"Sure and fine by me." He crushed out his smoke in the ashtray on the bar and took her hand.

The room was empty and the only sounds were the gusts of wind that occasionally played at the corner of the building as the night closed in around Clover Bay.

252

CHAPTER 30

The front page of the *Seattle Post-Intelligencer* exploded with four excellent photographs. The headline read "Unidentified Flying Object Over Useless Bay." The story that went with it had been picked up by AP and CNN on the morning edition. Experts were coming out of the woodwork on at least three national television systems, explaining how this could not be a saucer. Yet, the public had seen it and live broadcasts from Clover Bay were being scheduled by mid-morning.

Three vans had rolled into town and news crews were setting up to do live remotes back to Atlanta and New York. Folks were being asked all kinds of questions. Over at the barbershop, Harv was almost hoarse from talking to strangers. Mildred had not sold so many knickknacks and postcards since the summer of '63, when the storm hit Alaska, and Clover Bay was used for a field station for the U.S.G.S. and Red Cross.

One of the first interviews was with Clyde

Lindsey. As the only lawyer in Clover Bay, everyone in the news business thought he could complete a sentence and not sound like a damn fool. The preliminaries had been simple. Don't look at the camera. Talk to the reporter, and just talk about what you saw and what impact it has had on the town. The lead-in was quick and the cameraman motioned that they were live to Atlanta. The reporter was about forty, sandy-haired with a receding hairline and a mustache. He spoke with a matter-of-fact manner that implied to everyone in the listening and viewing audience that this was just one more human interest story to him. The report was to be for no more than sixty seconds.

"This is Ted Jesco in Clover Bay, Washington coming to you live. With me is Clyde Lindsey, a local attorney and witness to last night's aerial phenomenon. Mr. Lindsey, can you tell me what you saw?"

"It was about five thirty. Out of the east, there was a loud electrical sound — like a sparking sound. Over the tree line we, the community here, saw a small circular craft moving at high speed. It came toward the house where we were, and seemed to be spinning and giving off a lot of light and sound. It flew past us and headed west. It started to climb and then went supersonic and was gone."

"Do you think it was an experimental aircraft or just a jet that was too low? A lot of people get confused when they see those things up close."

"That is probably true. But...." Before the reporter could respond, Clyde had pulled out an enlarged photo of the craft. Tesla had made it for him early that morning and left it on the sideboard before he departed for Seattle. "This is a photo one of the locals took, and as you can see, it is not a jet or other type of 'known' aircraft. Nope, it was a UFO and we got proof. Photos, tape recordings of the sounds, and nearly a hundred eyewitnesses."

"Well, I see." The cameraman had panned in on the photo and was showing it to twenty million viewers —live. "Perhaps...ah...."

"This is the real thing. The thing that former President Carter and many others talked about. This is a spacecraft from some other world and they have come to Clover Bay."

The cameraman motioned to the reporter that Atlanta was on his headset telling him to continue the interview. They wanted more, and right now. Taken by surprise, the reporter landed on his feet well. "This could be a joke, could it not, Mr. Lindsey?"

"If it is, it is on the American people. Better yet, the people of the world. This is proof of the existence of alien intelligence. I would expect that the government will try to close this whole place up within hours just to stop the story from spreading. But no one can keep serious researchers and the common man from coming here and trying to find out for themselves what really happened."

"Well, yes. But that sounds to me like you don't believe that the government will want to find out the truth."

"The government is already here. Take a look

over there. Can you move the camera to see those two guys in the suits over at the barbershop? They showed up yesterday and have been asking at lot of questions. Watch this." Cupping his hands around his mouth and directing his voice toward the men in question, he hollered, "Hey, you two. Come over here." The cameraman followed as Lindsey started to walk toward Stewart and the other. They started to walk away trying to keep their faces from the camera. Then Lindsey stopped and turned back to the camera.

"They are working out of the Sheriff's office one block over, and won't tell anybody who or what they are. Isn't that just interesting as all hell? We get hit with a flying saucer that almost kills one of our finest deputy sheriffs, and now the government is here and won't talk. Do you really think this is a joke?"

The camera swung back to the reporter. "Well, no…I don't. We are returning back to our anchor, but we will have updates throughout the day for CNN…."

Lindsey had walked away and was heading for Dixie Raye's. Ace was standing on the front porch. "Nice job, counselor. It would seem as if you were born to raising hell. But there may be a problem." He pointed toward the news crew that was now talking to an Indian that had just walked out of Mildred's place with a plastic bag in both hands.

"Oh shit." Lindsey went white.

"It's the little things that make life interesting, Clyde." Ace turned and walked back into the restaurant. Lindsey stood and watched the interview happening.

Lothak pointed to the sky and waved his arms. "Oh shit...."

. . . . .

Stewart was back at the CNC in the Sheriff's substation when the light on the flash communicator went on. It pulsed twice before he picked up the handset.

"Clover Bay. Duty Officer Stewart here."

"Nice job. Did you go to school to learn how to screw up this well, or does it just come naturally. This is just great! I'm sitting here in this rented house on Pennsylvania Avenue watching people that I employ to do one job and they're doing just the opposite. Just what do you plan to do now that half the voters west of the Mississippi know that there is a 'real-life flying saucer' working the west coast?"

"I was going to call Fallon and request a Phase Four Alert and call the local Navy base and shut this place down for ten days." Stewart was grabbing at straws in the wind.

"You can't do that, you dummy. It is out now, and the more we try to suppress it, the more they will know that we are involved. Discredit it you asshole! Get Hargrove up there and make some kind of scientific statement about something. Find out what the hell and where the hell that thing went. And do it now!"

The line went dead again. Stewart sat back and closed his eyes for a minute. This was not going the way it was suppose to — at all.

· · · · ·

Clyde was sitting in the bar watching the news program and the flickering images coming in from around the world. Then he saw the same reporter that he had talked to earlier on screen again. "Turn it up, Ace. This could be...," he silenced himself with one look from Ace.

The old Indian with his white hair and stoic features was looking toward the reporter. The sound picked up just after the lead-in. "...What exactly did you see Mr. Lothak?"

"A fiery brother from the night sky."

"Then you say that you saw it also, is that correct?"

"Yes. Last night my boy and I were fishing on the Bay. Cold night. But there was a fiery sky-brother over the Bay."

"You make it sound like you have see them here before, is that true?"

"Many times. My people have known about them for hundreds of years. We never talk to others because white people will think that we are drunks or mad. So we keep this information to ourselves. But they come from a great distance. They are probably the same ones that come from Zeta Reticulum. They have been here many times. We have seen their star charts. But...," he turned and walked away without another word.

"Well, this is interesting. More eyewitnesses to this event. Back to you, Greg, at News Center."

The set went directly to a commercial about some kind of handy wipe for kitchen spills.

"I'll be damned!" Lindsey sat transfixed as Ace turned down the sound on the set.

"Doubt that, Counselor, but you can't assume too much these days." Ace was smiling. It was the first time in days Lindsey had seen him do that.

"Why do you think?"

WAYNE E. HALEY

CHAPTER 31

All morning Mallory had been pacing back and forth between the computers and the scope on the porch. He was using a small hand-held calculator and continually puffing on his pipe. He pulled off the printout and spread it out on the table. "Jesus, Mary, and Joseph!"

He hurried to the phone in the parlor, quickly punched in the number at Dixie Raye's and asked to speak with Ace. "If you and Lindsey are there, get here...now!" He hung up without waiting for a reply. He headed to the large dining room and looked in. Lady Lydia was sitting at the table reading a book. "It's time, Your Ladyship. Find Haddoxes and man, er... I mean person your station."

"Are you sure, Doc?"

"Oh yeah, I'm sure! It is bigger than my instruments can read. If those jerks try to close the breach this time, they'll rip a hole in space that half the Beta Gamma fleet could come through. Line abreast!"

He turned and headed back to the parlor.

Quickly and smoothly, she moved up the stairs and to the room where she had placed the transceiver. When she got there, Haddoxes already had it on and was sending out an array of signals.

"Well, old friend, let's see if anybody out there is paying attention." She sat down next to the small desk and watched the face-shifter. He had abandoned his cat-like guise and had transitioned into his primary shape. Grunting, he intently worked the dials.

CHAPTER 32

By the time the group had assembled in the parlor, it was late Monday afternoon. The newspapers on the west coast had carried morning and afternoon editions about the sighting. News crews had exhausted all possible information sources, and Clover Bay had taken on a new air of distinction. Most of the people in the community were strangely proud that they were part of something that suddenly commanded national attention.

The reality was that few, with the exception of those in Margaret Twitchell's old living room, realized what was really happening directly over them in the obscure recess of the space-time continuum. The rip in the fabric, started forty some years before, was opening the world to the possibility of alien contact of the fourth kind. It was the direct and real face-to-face kind of contact with folks that would not be happy to be blasting along at hyperspeed and suddenly find themselves dropped into a space-and-time hole that led them to

Clover Bay, Washington.

Among them was Giady, the Chronicler of the Tissen Confederation on Delta Epsolan Four, in the third dacmir of the regent Haarikod. It had been pointed out that nearly two-thirds of the sentient beings in the universe were relatively friendly to each other, if for no other reason than mutual commerce.

It was the other third that everybody in the known universe worried about. It was this same third that Mallory worried about so much. He had learned over years of research that few, if any, members of the secret government project knew about the collection of life forms that inhabited the universe. They were of the belief that there were a few isolated advanced races, but that those folks were in the minority. They really had no way of analyzing the total confederation, since most of the *visitors* they had under raps were either dead or not willing to communicate from an isolation tank. Understandably so.

"Well, how are the charming streets of Clover Bay doing today, Clyde?" Mallory had seated himself at the computer console and was studying printouts while he spoke.

"There are a lot more people than normal. The papers in Seattle did a good job of spreading the word. This afternoon's ferry had nearly a hundred-and-fifty people on it. They have filled the motel and the hotel. Mildred is doing a business that she has only had orgasmic dreams about in the past. Dixie ain't doing too bad either; she has had to call the mainland to have them ship in extra food and drink to handle the rush. From what I can glean from the idle chatter is that most of these folks are either researchers, amateur or professional, and then a lot of looky-loos that just want to see if they can spot a real saucer." He looked around at the collection of people that he now classified as friends. It was a new sensation to him. He had been quick to accept them all and found that he felt more comfortable with them than any group he had ever been around.

"This is good. It will lend to the general confusion and give those government jerks a little more to worry about than just the residents of this hamlet." Mallory's eyes drifted to the windows, his thoughts lost in an inner rumble of questions. "The principal thing that we must accomplish is to keep the pressure on them."

"Yup, and that means another run." Ace was thumbing through a copy of *Popular Science.*

"Well, I'm not so sure...." Mallory was showing the concern and tiredness from three solid days and nights of monitoring the instruments and computers.

Lindsey had noticed that Mallory's joviality had waned. This was a serious business to him and Lindsey knew that there was a lot riding on it.

"Have to. There are enough people and news crews lingering around that it would seem prudent to take that little piece of wire and fabric back out and give it another run — down the Bay this time." Ace had put down the magazine and looked at each member of the group. "It only makes sense."

Tesla was signing and Mallory watched carefully.

Tesla looked at Ace and back to Mallory. Mallory was nodding his head in agreement. "He's right. He says that you may get one more run out of it, but he is concerned that it won't hold if you try more than that."

"She was a little shaky on the first one, but I figure that if I keep her level and gentle in the banks and turns, she should hold together." Lindsey noted the worry around the eyes of the pilot.

"What happens if she doesn't?" Lindsey heard the words before he realized that they had come from himself.

"That thing has the aerodynamic glidepath of a '56 Buick." Ace had a twisted smile on his lips. "If I lose lift, it is going to fall like an anvil, and the impact on the Bay is going to break it into about a half-a-billion pieces."

"You too?" Lindsey didn't like the prospect of losing someone he had grown fond of lately. He already had to deal with losing Lady Lydia as her impending departure neared.

"Well, it has to do with Newton's second and third laws. They deal with resting and moving bodies and what happens when inertia takes hold. I won't need a tombstone; let's just leave it at that." Ace was pulling out one of his, by now, familiar smokes.

"Then why do it? It sounds like there's more risk than it is worth." Lindsey felt that old creeping sensation of his youth returning to him — the one about caution always being the better path.

"'Cause it needs doing. We started this to help some folks and that's what we intend to do. Risk doesn't matter. It's like a mountain climber being halfway up the Matterhorn. He can't just say 'screw this' halfway up, 'cause he's still got to go back down no matter what. So, he might as well see what the top looks like."

Someplace in all of that there was logic, but Clyde just failed to see it. He turned to Mallory and started to speak. Mallory's upheld hand brought him to a halt.

"Enough talk. We go at seven tonight." He looked at Ace who was shaking his head and then at Tesla, who signed quickly and shook his head also.

"Do you know how crazy this sounds. You're worried that the thing won't work and yet you'll still try it. And if it doesn't work, you will all be responsible for Ace's demise." Lindsey was using his best "L.A. Law" voice and trying to sound authoritarian.

"Ace is responsible for Ace. Nobody is going to put a knife in my back and tell me to go fly that bird. I am doing it because that's the thing I need to do. These folks will do what they need to do and hopefully those fools from the government will follow suit. And if we're all really lucky, Lady Lydia and Haddoxes will get their shot at success and nothing will come through that sky hole to render this whole exercise meaningless." Ace was looking directly at Lindsey. Lindsey had that feeling again of the remiss school boy that had just wet his pants in class and had been detected by the teacher.

"What can we do?" The voice was from the doorway. The old Indian and his son stood there and looked at the room full of people. Lothak was sipping on a Diet Pepsi and Michael was consuming one of the sandwiches that had been on the sideboard. Nobody knew how long they had been standing there.

"Er...well..." Lindsey suddenly felt responsible for them and their knowing about the plan.

"Lothak, you old pirate. Get in here. I saw you on the telly and you did the best Shitting Bull routine I've ever seen!" Mallory was laughing and walked over and slapped a handshake on the old Indian. Michael gnawed away and brandished a nearly toothless smile to Mallory, who motioned toward the sideboard. Michael took another sandwich, put it on a plate and piled some chips next to it from the bag.

"You know each other?" Lindsey was standing and looking as if he just found out that the names on his birth certificate were not his own parents.

"Sure, long time." Lothak came over to the overstuffed divan and sat next to Angel. "You still following the Jesus road, little sister?"

"Yah, yah. And so should you, you ugly heathen." She slapped the old Indian on his thigh.

"Higher and to the left," he winked at her and she pushed him in play. "Looks like Wounded Knee around this town. Feds, news people, and tourists. Maybe the tribe should start an uprising to help out."

"No, I don't think so. Besides, you guys have no complaints. You got land, fishing rights, government subsidies, and all the beer that you can drink sold to you at outrageous prices in Clover Bay. What more could you want?" Mallory was playing with his pipe.

"Our ancestral lands back." Lothak looked around at the people and then started to laugh. "Or a bingo parlor on the reservation to fleece fat old tourist ladies out of their social security checks. We will call the numbers out in Indian. That way the whites can't win."

"You're still a rascal, and at your age." Mallory was overdoing the shaking of the head.

"How is the Dark Lady and her friend?" Lothak turned suddenly serious.

"She desires to go home and see family," Mallory answered, to Clyde's amazement, like they were talking about going down to Tacoma for the weekend.

"Been too long for her. Not good at all for people to be away from loved ones this long." Lothak pulled out a small cigar and lit it. "She needs to see her mate and friends."

The world inside Lindsey's head erupted like Mt. Fuji in the fifteenth century. The stuff he thought of as gray matter just boiled into the cracks in his skull, and most of what he thought of as reality went into hyperdrive. "Her mate?" Lindsey was standing and speaking to nobody in general.

"Whoops," Ace began whistling through his teeth.

"Nice job, Lothak." Mallory turned and buried his face in a computer printout.

"Mate?" Lindsey found himself caught in a causality loop.

"Different worlds, different customs," Angel said.

"Mate!" This time the words seemed almost a whisper.

"I think it's time for a 'come-to-Jesus' talk, old pard." Ace had taken Clyde's arm and was directing him toward the front door. They walked down the steps and out toward the shore. All the time Mallory watched as Ace talked. He knew the speech that was being given.

"He seems to suffer from Temporal Discontinuity and PPD." Lothak had walked over and gotten himself a sandwich and some black olives.

"Sometimes. It comes and goes." Mallory had put a stack of printouts next to the Indian's seat. "Take a look."

"Light fog tonight. Come about six and stay till about one. It will be just over the water to about two hundred feet. If we're gonna make the run, Ace needs to keep the Wasp at about a hundred feet. The ground effect will buffet him, but if he gets too high he will have trouble getting a fix on the water and could overshoot his glidepath and crash in the water." It was the first time Michael had spoke. "He's got to watch the left stabilizer also, it was shaking really bad the other night. If he turns hard into it, it will snap like a twig."

"I could realign it." Angel was looking at her drawings.

"No time," Mallory was looking at the computer.

"The hole open?" Lothak was reading the printout.

"About three hours so far." Mallory was punching keys on the left computer.

"Hmm...the Dark Lady on her communicator?" Lothak looked up from the printout and then returned to them.

"Should be. She or Haddoxes." Mallory turned back to the group.

Tesla was signing again. "You're right. He says that more Feds will be here soon now that the event is happening."

"I would say that tonight's the night, Doc." Lothak put down the papers and got up. "Me and Michael will get the boat ready and be on the Bay as soon as possible."

"Good, and...thanks," Mallory stood.

"No need. It has to be done." With that, Lothak and Michael walked out into the night.

Ace sauntered back inside, chuckling to himself. "Well, there will be a few words exchanged later, I would imagine. It seems like our Lady just fails to point out all the facts sometimes, doesn't she?"

"As Angel said, different places, different customs." Mallory flipped on the scanner that Tesla had hooked up. It started to scan the government restricted frequencies. At present all seemed pretty quiet. "Tonight. In about an hour, Ace. Fast run, down the slot, over the Harbor and then run for the barn. Angel? You and Tesla get down there and be ready to take the Wasp apart as fast as you can. Ace, when you're through, get back to Dixie's and act like you have been there all night. Lothak and Michael will be on the Bay if anything goes..." Mallory stopped in mid-sentence as Clyde came back into the room.

"Where do you want me, Doc?" Lindsey, with a

little insight from Ace into Stygian customs, had regained his composure and had been able to put things back into perspective.

"If you're up to it, get back into town and make sure that a lot of the tourists and townsfolk are looking out at the Bay at seven. It is necessary that as many as possible see tonight's little show." Mallory tossed him the keys to the Dodge and turned back to the computer.

"Ah...roger." With that, he was out the door and running to the car.

"Roger, who?" Mallory turned and looked into the empty room.

CHAPTER 33

Philip Stewart had driven up to the NAS at the top of the island and had picked up Hargrove and his two assistants. It had been a quiet drive and he had been rehearsing his speech. It sounded okay to him, but this was always the way. He knew that Hargrove would not let him finish a complete sentence. Phillips had decided that Hargrove, for all his genial appearance, was not a friendly person at all.

Dr. Edward Hargrove had been with Firestorm since it was formed in the late forties. It was his project. He had inherited it from Neuman, Brown, and Einstein. He had built it up during good times and bad. It had been the most successful long-term project in the government's history, mostly because of the secrecy connected to it.

He had been there at its birth and he was planning to stay with it until they finally shut that damn wormhole in the sky. He had almost lost it during the Carter

Administration when the peanut farmer had wanted to go public. But Hargrove had called in enough old markers and friends to put enough pressure on the old boy to shut him up and make him go off and build houses for the poor. Hargrove had liked the last few years, because every time he went up to Washington and asked for something to improve the operation of Firestorm, he got it. The old Gipper had loved it. It worked hand-in-glove with S.D.I. and that made everything better.

But this one was going to be the first real test. He had the new Siva Laser in orbit. Nobody knew it. Congress didn't, the Soviet's didn't, and most of the government didn't. Only the Shrub and a close-knit group of specialists that had worked for nearly ten years at Lawrence Livermore knew it. It was ready. When the hole showed up, they would fire a bolt of over ten million joules of electro-magnetic energy into it. The thing would close up and go away forever. And he could lay to rest those three old bastards that had started this whole mess fifty years ago. It had taken nearly two years of planning just to get the right combination of items, put their prize on a shuttle, have a crew launch it and not know what the hell it was. He truly believed that he had accomplished the greatest feat in scientific history and nobody would know. Too bad. It was at least worth a Nobel Prize, but sometimes fate doesn't quite go the way one would like it to.

Stewart was rattling off something about why and how as they drove back to the little town down the coast. Hargrove was half listening and fiddling with the heater knob to get more warm air into the car. Stewart was talking about not having a window of opportunity when the first sighting was made, and that all the instruments indicated that it should not have happened.

Hargrove wondered why he could not have all scientists on his team, but the guys in the executive branch wanted to make sure that the team was staffed with trained field agents. Hargrove always wondered what these guys were trained in. He knew it was neither science, nor was it public relations.

The portable cellular phone went off. Hargrove picked it up, "Hargrove."

"A major event has just started at sixteen-forty-two Pacific. There are no present indicators of any occurrences, but the bird's position is about four hours and twelve minutes to arrival over sight for lock and initiation."

"Clear." Hargrove pushed the button on the phone that closed down the circuit. It would take the small thruster jets four hours and twelve minutes to position the Siva directly over the path of the wormhole. He had planned it this way so that he would get the maximum benefit of the laser as it punched its way into the hole. Some had suggested that it could be fired from any position. But Hargrove had feared that the power lost from the bloom would affect the closure. He wanted to hit the hole once and not have to do it again. He also believed that if the Siva was directly in the path of the wormhole, it might be caught in the hole. If so, it could become overloaded and explode, having the same effect.

The net effect would still be closing the hole forever. Two chances to win. Now all that was left was the waiting and hoping that nothing showed up in the hole for the next two hours. The initiation would take place at seven-thirty local time. He pulled his collar up around his ears and listened to Stewart go on about why he had called earlier for a Phase Three clean up.

CHAPTER 34

Mallory had listened carefully to the scanner as the emotionless voice had reported to somebody that they were going to be ready for the pulse to happen at 7:30. He looked at his chronograph. It would be cutting it close for Ace to make his run. If nothing else, the light show in the upper atmosphere would make Clover Bay a landmark for years to come. That is, if Clover Bay was still here when some damn fool pulsed a million-volt laser directly into an area of space that would do nothing but amplify it a million times. "How could anybody be stupid enough not to know what to expect when this thing went off?" Mallory mumbled to himself. These guys had to be working alone and not talking to anybody else. Otherwise they would have calculated this all differently.

He shut down the computers and unplugged each of them from the wall sockets. The pulse of electro-magnetic energy would cause all electrical devices to fail.

This included cars, computers, televisions, radios, and especially the electrical systems on aircraft.

He walked over and turned out the lights. He positioned his chair in the window. It was going to be an interesting night.

Lady Lydia moved into the room silently. She reached down and put her hand on his shoulder. He reached up and put his over hers. "Something?"

"Haddoxes found an outpost ship working the quadrant. It took some time to explain what had happened. They called for instructions and the high council ordered them to make the run, the wormhole run. They were not keen on the idea, but they will be here within the hour. Haddoxes is making everything ready."

"There may be a problem." He kept his voice as flat as possible.

"No, don't tell me this is the one." She tightened her grip on his shoulder.

"Then I won't tell you that in less than an hour, those bozos are going to punch Siva on-line and pulse it, right above us." He reached around and pulled her down to sit on the arm of the chair. "If your folks are slow, or of faint heart, they are going to be in the middle of one of the greatest time distortion experiments ever tried. If you get on that ship, you may end up on the other side of the universe or in a dimension from which there is no return." Mallory pulled at his beard.

"What should I do, Doc? Miss a chance because of a risk factor?" She was looking out into the night sky.

"If they're through by 7:20 and you can get on and get out by then, go. But any longer and the risk is too great. I wouldn't want you to try it. Besides, if they pulse that thing, we are going to have plenty of opportunities in the near future." He tried to sound confident. "Except there might not be a planet Earth in the future if that hole opens up any more than it already has and somebody comes to dinner that you're not expecting."

She sensed the tightness in his stomach. She knew about worlds that had been visited by others. Some found they had no defense system to match the visitor's advance technology. "It would make the Cathar Wars look like child's play, Doc."

"Sure would," he did not need to think too much about it. She had been his first and best source of information about the death and destruction following discovery of non-advanced planets by the predatory races that moved through the galaxy.

"Lindsey wasn't doing well tonight. Lothak slipped. He accidently told him that you had a mate back on Stygian." Mallory looked at his watch again.

"So, I have a mate. I haven't seen him for years. What — is this some form of primitive jealousy I must contend with?" Her body tensed.

"He doesn't understand your people's ways. That's all." He wished he had never mentioned it, but it seemed a better subject than talking about genocide.

"I should speak with him and explain that I am a Mensuh. I am allowed to have a mate and others." She was speaking as if she was in the royal court.

"Think of him as a provincial — simple, bucolic in nature, almost banal. He can't help it. It is just his nature to feel that there is something important between you two. I think he loves you." Mallory pulled his pipe out and started to fill it.

"Probably. Why wouldn't he. I am wonderful."

Mallory started to laugh and coughed to the point of tears. "Yes, you are. And humble, too."

"Why should I be. I know that half the Tressiden Worhack would give their Bathmares to sleep with me for one night. Jentap offered my father a complete star system for that privilege. It was a small star system of only ten occupied planets and only a couple of billion slaves, but still...," she sat there as if her conversation was as normal as if she was talking about going over to Mildred's to buy some Dove bars.

"Anyway, take some pity on the boy and don't be too upset if he gets a little green around the gills." Mallory picked up his binoculars and started to watch out over the Bay.

"That's if I ever see him again, Doc. If things go according to plan, I will be out of here in less than forty minutes." She hesitated and rubbed his shoulder, "So, I guess that I need to say..."

"You need to say nothing, my dear. We are, have been, and always will be good friends — wherever we are. You have a life and it's not here. We both knew or hoped that this day would come. I have spent twelve years on this project, preparing for the day when you could go home. I have and always shall love you in my own way.

So, don't try to make it easier. It won't be. For either of us. But right now, it is time to get ready." He stood up and turned to look at her.

"Now who is not humble?" Her blue-within-blue eyes gleamed in the dark of the old room.

"No need. I know that this is not the end for us. Somehow there will be another meeting between us. If not here, then out there, perhaps?" He pointed with his pipe stem toward the sky.

"Being metaphysical are we?"

"Always!" He walked over to the desk, turned on the lamp and looked at the printout one last time. "Now, get Haddoxes and be ready. Where is the meet to happen?"

"On the shoreline in front of the house." She pointed to the shore that stretched between Margaret Twitchell's old house and the water of Useless Bay.

"Best to be going, My Lady." He turned and saw Haddoxes in the room. He was holding the transceiver and the small black leather case that Lady Lydia always had in her vehicle with her. He knew that it carried the genetic map that demonstrated her rightful place as a possible heir to the throne of Stygia. Haddoxes had returned to his form as a guild navigator with his green skin and bony hide. His pink eyes stared at Mallory. "I knew you were a sheep-stealing son-of-a-bitch. Now get her Ladyship ready before I have Ace parboil you into a stew."

Mallory turned so as not to allow either of them to see the tears in the corners of his eyes. It had been a long time, and he had grown very used to his old friends.

"Backta Thenocl Haddoxes," Haddoxes put his hand someplace in the vicinity of his chest.

"Me too. Now get going." Mallory never turned back to them.

CHAPTER 35

Ace was sitting in the Wasp warming up the engines. He had been studying the vibration of the left stabilizer. Lothak and Michael were probably right — he shouldn't turn into it because of stress. So he had planned his flight to use only counter-stressing turns. Angel walked over, leaned into the cockpit, and motioned to her watch. Tesla had opened the doors to the old barn. The fog was light and that would make determining ground level, or in this case, water level, just that much harder. Ace signed to Tesla and he nodded in agreement.

Ace closed the canopy and slid the big black knob to the full forward position. The Wasp lurched up and then forward. By the edge of the beach, Ace had put the spurs to it and the Wasp started to move faster and faster. The fog was pushing around the Plexiglas and giving Ace a sense of being inside a Wilson Cloud Chamber.

He looked at the illuminated dial on his watch

and noted that it was 7:21 as he started the downwind leg run toward Clover Bay. In two minutes he would pass the boat in the Bay that held Lothak and Michael. They would turn on a spotlight for only a second, but the light would collide with the fog long enough to be an indicator to him that it was time to switch on all the bells and whistles.

Clyde had collected about twenty people in front of the old Harbor and was talking to them about the history of Clover Bay and the recent experiences that had happened. It was not a big group, but he estimated that there needed to be some form of reality to this. He could not march a hundred people out and tell them to watch the night sky because the great fiery brothers were about to return. This seemed to be the best course.

Hargrove was sitting in the van monitoring the various instruments and reading the printout that was coming off the flash communicator's modem port. He was looking at the red digital clock built into the console when the flashing light came on, indicating flash traffic from Fallon. "Clover Bay, Hargrove."

"Occurrence. Two minutes ago. Directly over you. Beam-type ship, nuclear powered. High point marker one-hundred-thousand feet slowing to sub-atmospheric speed. Fallon out."

Hargrove put the handset back down. "Damn ...damn, not now!" He turned and looked at the computer screen. "Three minutes to mark. Continue countdown."

One of the other duty officers noticed the bleep

on the screen and pointed to it and looked at Hargrove without a word.

"Fortunes of war, my boy. Fortunes of war. Continuing countdown."

• • • • •

Ace passed the beam of light that flashed from below. He switched on the generator, halogen lights, and tape player within a second of each other. The halogen lights bloomed in the fog and blinded him for the most part. He would be flying on dead reckoning and instinct now. "This is where it gets a little tight, with a sphincter factor of twelve on a ten scale." He started to hum an old Marty Robbins tune about an Arizona ranger who wouldn't be too long in town.

Clyde fought the instinct to turn immediately when the first sound of the subwoofers came booming in from over the Bay. But the crowd started pointing and pulling up cameras. He finally turned and put his hand up to his mouth in his best Richard Carlson pose. "What is it? Could it be?"

"It's a saucer."

"Get the picture."

"Look at that...."

A myriad of voices all blended in. Lindsey looked at his watch. It was exactly 7:30. But then, he already knew that.

. . . . .

The Siva satellite had reached its new position three minutes early, but the coded instructions had been already set. The synchronizer in the bird had been tuned to the atomic clock at Boulder, Colorado. It was accurate within ten nanoseconds in a ten-year period. The download from Fallon had given the bird relative autonomy to conduct all primary functions, and at exactly zero three thirty Zulu time, fire a one-millisecond pulse of highly coherent light containing a million joules of electromagnetic energy. FAA had diverted all aircraft out of the area for the past hour with a claim that there were Naval Operations going on. Emergency Broadcasting had put out a report that there was a severe electrical storm occurring in the upper atmosphere, and NOAA, the National Oceanic and Atmospheric Administration had done likewise. Palomar and Kitt Peak had received teletypes to confirm the upper atmosphere story or lose federal funding forever. Hargrove had promised that the pulse would only moderately disturb normal operations of electrical systems, and that everything would be back on-line within minutes. Northwestern Bell had been informed to put more operators on the switchboards because of the storm and all the calls that they would receive. The statisticians at Fallon had expected a four-hour gridlock of the normal communications channel in the northwest. All of this was put into the computer. This was the climax of forty some years of work.

· · · · ·

All of this didn't matter much to Ace when he was making his long slow turn to the right. He had just pulled out and hit the throttle again to accelerate back to the barn. He studied his compass and leaned as far forward as he could to get as much speed as the Wasp would produce. He looked at his stopwatch and noted that he had fifteen seconds to kill the generator and lights.

The sky exploded with an electrical blue shock wave. His complete nervous system responded and he pulled his body back and threw an arm up to cover his eyes. This action moved the center of gravity in the Wasp to the left and aft. This shearing effect was enough to place an instantaneous four g's of stress on the stabilizer near the left front section of the Wasp. It snapped with a roar. The Wasp pancaked end over end. The sudden movement pulled all of the blood out of Ace's head and straight to his feet. The inside of his skull went black.

Mallory had put on his welder's goggles and was watching. He jerked them off and looked at his chronograph. Seven twenty eight. "Jesus, Mary, and Joseph! The damn thing is out of sync!"

He could not see into the fog. But he instinctively knew that Ace would not yet have made it back to the barn. He needed one more minute.

Clyde was on the ground and had his head covered with his coat. The rest of the people were similar forms on the ground. Clover Bay was completely dark. Clyde was up and moving toward his office at a flat run. He knew he needed to get out to the old Twitchell place as fast as he could.

Hargrove watched the system come back up on-line as the emergency back-up power system in the van took over for the failed commercial power input. The flash communicator was lighting up. "Clover Bay, Hargrove."

"Pulse completed. Two occurrences in sector. One beam type and one of unknown origin. Pulse failed to close breach. Breach expanded by a factor of seven. Fallon clear."

Before Hargrove could respond, the flashing light was pulsing again on the box. "Yes?"

"Well, Doctor, what happened? It seems like all the bullshit you handed us was just that. They tell me that it didn't close the hole. You opened the thing up like a goddamn can opener. This is just going to be great."

"I need some time to study it, to calculate what went wrong, sir." Hargrove's mouth was dry and his chest tight.

"Time, mister, is what you don't have. You calculate all you want, but somebody better have some answers or else you're going to be running the science station in Antarctica...forever!" The line went dead.

CHAPTER 36

It had taken twenty minutes for the lights to come back on in Clover Bay. The grid had to be switched from eastern Oregon and routed through California for the utilities to compensate for the flux on the lines. It had taken five minutes more for phone lines and power to reach the old Twitchell place at the end of Bay Road.

Mallory was walking around turning on computers and starting to reset the programs to monitor the warp area. This would be the critical time. He needed to know how long the space-time warp would remain open and when it would close again. This would give him the information necessary to determine when the next breach would happen. He didn't want to think about the Wasp, or Ace, or anything else. He sat down and looked at the pipe in his hand. He noticed that his hand was shaking badly. The adrenaline was pumping through his veins at a tremendous rate. He fumbled for his lighter and it dropped to the floor. He reached down to pick it up and noticed a pair of yellow cat eyes looking at him. He looked a little further into the room and saw a pair of highly-polished black boots with legs that led up to a set of blue-within-blue eyes; they looked down at him quizzically. "You look like you never saw a Stygian before."

Haddoxes meowed and rubbed against Mallory. "I thought by now you would be a parsec from here."

"The detectors on the ship noted the pulse building in the satellite and they aborted the pickup. Prime directive. No loss of life no matter how important." She walked over to the computers and studied them. "Can you put up with me a little longer, Doc?"

"Oh, hell. I guess so, Your Ladyship." He sat back in his chair and felt a calm pass through his body. "What happened to the fellows in your ship?"

"I ordered them out before the pulse. They violated a general order and put it in hyperdrive while still in the atmosphere. It must have been a hell of a big show over L.A. tonight." Her eyes were sparkling.

"I can imagine. Hyperdrive in the atmosphere is always interesting to watch, to say the least."

She sat down next to him. She could feel his emotions as they poured into the room. "Did Ace make it?"

"I don't think so. The timing was too close. He needed another minute. But…," he turned with the acceptance of someone who knew reality for what it was.

The front door opened and closed. Clyde ran into the living room. "Lydia, you're still here.?" He was breathless and looked confused.

"Yes. Is that alright by you?"

"Of course. I was scared that you would have left already. I am...er...uh...glad that...," he tried to find his words.

"I'm still here, too," Mallory looked up and lit his pipe.

"I didn't expect you to be gone, Doc. I'm glad that you are here too." He reached down and picked up Haddoxes. "You sheep-stealing son-of-a-bitch! I am glad to see you, too, you little bastard." He rubbed the cat and played with it like a pet.

"If you could have seen him an hour ago, you would have gone white with fright. Now you look like you've just found Fluffy, your long lost kitten, for Christ's sakes." Mallory gazed out the window.

The cat meowed and rubbed itself into Lindsey's arms.

"Lydia?"

"Enough. We have time, but later." She walked over to Mallory and touched him. "It looks like Ace was killed in the Wasp."

The shock tore though Lindsey's mind. Trying to regain his composure, he stood motionless. "No, it couldn't be. I didn't see anything of the craft hitting the water. It would have shown up, wouldn't it have?" Lindsey walked out onto the deck.

"You okay, Doc?" There was genuine concern in her voice.

"Peachy...Your Ladyship...I'm sorry." He faced her

again, feeling weak and old.

"No reason to be. You and he have been together so long you could never believe that he wouldn't be here." She touched him and looked out the windows.

Lindsey was holding onto the rail that stretched around the porch.

Mallory and Lady Lydia were looking into the dark over Useless Bay. Haddoxes had curled up in a chair and was asleep. The old Twitchell place was silent with the exception of the humming of the computers and the ticking of the old grandfather clock in the hallway. Time seemed to be in abeyance.

"This place looks like a funeral parlor to me. What's up, somebody die?"

Lady Lydia and Mallory spun around. Lindsey burst in through the screen door. Ace was standing there, his flight suit soaked through; he was drinking a beer.

He tossed a D-ring across the room. It was about eight-inches long and had a cable attached to it. Mallory caught it in flight. He looked at it — a grand smile on his face.

"A little present from that crafty little Samurai. A ballistic chute added at the last minute. That thing deployed about two feet from the water. I was in the drink for ten seconds and Lothak and his boy played cowboys and Indians for real. Picked me up, attached two floatation rafts to the Wasp, and towed it over to the barn. Tesla and Angel are stripping it right now, and say they'll be done and crated by morning." He finished his beer and tossed the can into the trash basket next to the desk.

"Where are Lothak and Michael?" Mallory was looking around the room.

"Had to make it back to the reservation to catch the last half of Monday night football." Ace turned to see Lindsey just staring at him. "Counselor, we're not taking long hot showers into the deep night, no matter how good it is to see me."

"Er...yeah...well...," Lindsey had a smile that ran from ear to ear.

"Would Your Ladyship consider helping this poor lad in regaining his senses?" Ace turned and winked at Lady Lydia.

"It would be my pleasure." She walked up and took him by the arm and started to lead him away.

"Doc? When will it," he pointed to the ceiling, "close up again?"

Mallory turned to one of the computers. "Already started. It's bigger, but it won't last as long."

"Good!" He looked at Lydia for a moment and then back to Mallory, "I mean that's *good* for the earth, but there will be other openings, right? So that Lydia and Haddoxes...?"

"Come along, Clyde. It has been a trying day for some of us." Lady Lydia walked up the stairs with Lindsey in tow.

"The boy just will not learn, will he? She is going to put permanent damage on him one of these days." Ace pulled out a Camel and lit it up from Mallory's pipe.

"Serves him right. Never did believe in intraspecies relationships. It's not normal." Both men started to laugh.

CHAPTER 37

As Clyde Lindsey walked down the stairs, he saw Mallory shaking hands with an older man who was getting back into a black sedan. The car held two other occupants. Mallory walked back into the house as Lindsey was pouring a cup of coffee. "What was that all about?"

"That old fart is with the government. Seems like they're concerned with the occurrence. They do this now and then. They claim that they are from some department or other in the government, and that they need to buy people out to put in a new base or a laboratory or the like. In reality, they're trying to suppress the story and move people out of here. I just cut a deal to sell this place and make it into an historical landmark. Nice plaque, take down the fence, repaint it. You know."

"When?"

"Got to be out by the end of the week." He lit his pipe. "Boy, are these guys dumb. It's a Phase Three buy-out. They just paid me double what I bought the place for, improvements and all. Got Lothak and his boy jobs as park rangers here; they'll explain to tourists the history and talk about old Margaret Twitchell and the cranberry fields." He laughed and picked up a Danish.

"Where are you going?" Lindsey moved over to the computers.

"Why do you want to know?" Mallory just looked blankly at him.

"Oh, just wondering. No big thing," Lindsey was trying to figure out what all the symbols meant on the screen.

"Well, if it is any concern of yours, I will pack all this stuff up and ship it to New Mexico. It looks like that's the next place that an occurrence will happen — in about nine months. It will give me some time to write another book and get ready for the next event." Mallory walked over and turned off the computers.

"Somebody say New Mexico?" Ace walked in and poured a cup of coffee. He had tossed a leather suitcase down and flung his flight jacket on top of it.

"Yeah. What of it?" Mallory was pulling out RS 232 plugs from the back of the computers.

"Whereabouts?" Ace sipped the coffee.

"Near Deming, south of it to be exact." Mallory was folding up printouts.

"Did either of you see Lydia this morning?" Lindsey looked between the two men.

"Oh, yeah," Mallory reached into his pocket and pulled out a letter. "She thought it was getting a little too hot around here, so she and Haddoxes took off. They decided to take Angel back to Seattle and then stroll around awhile before heading to New Mexico. She left this for you." Mallory handed him the letter and went back to work on the computers.

"Without saying good-bye?" Lindsey turned the letter in his hand.

"She's not good at saying good-bye. Part of her nature doesn't like long farewells."

"Oh. Well, I just thought...," Lindsey started.

"Shouldn't think. It seems like that's not a part of you that you ought to use, Counselor," Ace was grinning. "Got's to go. Be seeing ya."

"Where are you going, Ace?" Lindsey turned and looked directly at Ace.

"Got to head down to the southwest. Got a job training flight students for awhile." He pulled on his flight jacket and picked up his bag.

"New Mexico?'" Lindsey asked.

"Could be. Doc, give my best to that slant-eyed son of the east. Probably be seeing you one of these days, Doc." Ace moved toward the door.

"Great. Just what I am looking forward to." Mallory walked over and embraced the man. "Keep that cycle straight up. Hope you can ride it better than you can a Wasp!"

"Oh, sure! See ya two." He walked out and swung a leg over the Harley-Davidson and kicked it into life.

"Well, ah, I guess I need to head back to my office."

"Okay. Listen, Clyde, I will stop by and drop off

some papers for Hargrove and those other bozos from the government in a couple of hours." Mallory was loading up some boxes.

"Do you need some help?" Lindsey felt the moment slipping past him.

"No. You better grab Ace and get a ride into town."

"Oh. Yeah," he turned back and handed Mallory the keys to his Dodge station wagon. "I have grown used to that car."

"It grows on you, doesn't it?"

"Yeah...well," he turned and walked out. Ace had been sitting there waiting for him.

"Hold on, Counselor. Old Paint gets a little wild when he knows we're a-goin' for a ride." With that, he twisted the throttle and they took off down the old leaf-lined drive.

· · · · ·

Mallory had just finished packing the last of the computer gear and L'Amour books into the back of the station wagon when Tesla pulled up in his Mercedes. He signed from the driver's seat.

"Yes and probably," Mallory grinned past his pipe. "I do too, Mr. Tesla, but each to his own way, as the Buddha says. See you in New Mexico?"

Tesla made a group of signs and smiled.

"Good, and after you pick it up, bring it with you

and we will play with it. We'll have some time. See you there." Tesla pulled out into the lane and drove slowly down the road.

Mallory stood there looking at the old house. He liked this place, but work called and the new book was going around inside his mind. He really wanted to write another one about "The Cult of Silence" and how they had affected the lives of people for the past fifty years or so. He walked over and pulled down the tri-colored Stygian flag and respectfully folded it up. He walked back to his car and placed it inside a plastic case. It would appear again at the next embassy of the Stygian Triangle.

He pulled out his pipe and filled it. He surveyed the old place one more time and then slid into the driver's seat of the Dodge station wagon and started the engine.

• • • • •

Ace had just dropped Clyde off at his office and they had said their farewells. "Write, call, keep in touch." "Sure, you bet," and then Ace motored up the street slowly and stopped in front of Dixie Raye Russell's diner and lit up a Camel. Harv walked over and looked down at him from the sidewalk.

"Did you hear the news, Ace?"

"No, what's that, Harv?"

"Old fellow came in and bought up most of the commercial buildings in town. Said they were going to make a National Park here. But it don't make no sense,"

Harv added, rubbing his bald head.

"Why's that?" Ace found himself mildly interested for he had seen a buy-out before. Most people were just really happy.

"The paper." Harv handed him the *Seattle Post-Intelligencer.* The small box on the lower left-hand side carried a report that next Friday would see the last ferry service from Seattle to Clover Bay. The owners had decided not to continue service because of declining profits.

"Well ain't that something." He handed the paper back to Harv who looked at it and just kind of shuffled off.

"Well, I'll be damned." Dixie Raye was standing there in a pair of jeans and an old football letterman's jacket looking down at Ace. "I thought you had hit and run." She was holding a small traveling bag.

"Going someplace?" He looked up and down at her.

"Guy walked in this morning. Bought the diner for four times what it is worth. Wired the money into my Dad's account in Sand Point by eleven. I told him he could have everything but my clothes. He agreed and I took some folks advice about taking the money and running." She looked at him for a long minute. "Somehow, I didn't think I was going to see you again, Cowboy."

"Why is that?" He grinned his best Evel Knievel grin. "Something about laying and leaving I've just grown used to, I guess." She fought back a smile.

"No way. Told ya, you can take it to the bank, Lady," he leaned forward and kicked Old Paint to life again.

"Where ya headed?" She spoke above the bike's roar.

"New Mexico. Got some students to show how to fly birds." He crushed out his smoke and zipped up his jacket. He pointed to the bag she was holding. "You got anything in there you can't live without?"

"My toothbrush."

"Can always buy one of those on the road."

She dropped the bag on the deck, stepped onto the Harley and put her arms around him. "This is a strange way to propose to me, Cowboy. Or is it a proposition?"

"It's a match made in heaven, Dixie Raye. You know it and so do I, so let's not waste time. We got fifteen-hundred miles to talk about who gets to be bridesmaid and best man." He gunned the bike into life and they shot out of town past Deputy Bob, who was trying to finish the report he planned to drive up to the Sheriff's Office the next day. He looked up and automatically waved at them as they passed. "I'll get you yet for speeding," he went back to the report sitting on his knee in the car.

· · · · ·

The Dodge station wagon pulled up in front of Clyde Lindsey's office. When the doors opened, the street was filled with the sounds of the Beatles singing about "Maxwell's Silver Hammer."

Mallory waited until the last of the tune finished, pushed the "Eject" button on the tape player, and stepped from the car. Pounding his pipe on the post outside the office, he walked into Clyde's environment.

"Well, Counselor, it seems as though all that could be done has been done, and as the old poem says 'there are strange things done in the midnight sun.'" Mallory stood there looking down at Clyde.

"You're leaving?"

"It's time. 'A rolling stone…' and all that rot. I have a good idea for a book. So I think I'll drive down the coast and make notes on it then swing over to New Mexico and set up shop." Mallory pulled out three books from under his arm and handed them to Lindsey. "I thought you might like to read one of them."

"I would and I shall." Lindsey got up, took the books and walked out of the office.

"Uh…," Mallory walked out behind him and watched as Lindsey picked up a bag and tossed it in the back of the station wagon along with two books of law. He proceeded to walk around and get into the passenger's seat of the car. Mallory looked back and saw that the keys to the front door were in the lock, hanging there. He walked over and got into the driver's seat. "Just what do you think that you are doing?"

"You drive for awhile and I'll read. Then I'll drive and you make notes." Lindsey had started reading the book. "Makes perfect sense to me." He handed Mallory the letter from Lady Lydia. All it said was:

'See you in New Mexico.
— Lydia'

"I ain't putting up with no free loaders, Counselor," Mallory hit the starter.

"The way you live, you need an in-residence attorney. And I am a good attorney."

"We'll see."

The streets of Clover Bay were filled with the muffled sounds of the Beatles playing "Abbey Road" as the green 1950 Dodge station wagon sped down the street. Wibley, which was now a National Historical Park, silently braced itself for a cold, wet Washington winter.

The End